Tales  ....

"A great read from beginning to end. I can only hope there will be a Part III."
Stan Trollip
*Co-authored four books with Michael Sears, including
the Barry Award winning Death of the Mantis*

"This collection of short stories by a variety of talented writers will delight lovers of ghostly tales. From a 1920s train accident, to an avid knitter who receives help from a mysterious woman, to a ghost who is in love with a café owner, each story is charming, entertaining, and at times even creepy. *Tales from Two-Bit Street and Beyond* is a perfect blend of thrills and surprises."

Heather B. Moore
Whitney Award Winning Author

"Great stories with a bit of history thrown in and a good scare... From ghosts to ghouls to pranksters, and malevolent spirits, *Tales* will make you take a second look around a dark corner at night, perhaps have you spitting over your left shoulder... even say a prayer. Enter a world where reality meets other dimensions in a kaleidoscope of colors, each weaving a good, old-fashioned spooky yarn..."

Barbara Passaris
Award-winning author, Through Tempest Forged

"I thoroughly enjoyed *Tales*. It gave me goose-bumps. And the story of Joan, I'd like to say it was one of my favorites. The story was so sweet and tender. It brought tears to my eyes and shivers up and down my spine. The whole book was a real good read. All the authors did a great job!"

Janet Battisti
Avid reader with over 800 reviews on Goodreads

"The Two-Bit Street Writers are back again. Get ready for fresh thrills and chills along with a compelling glimpse of the history of a unique street in a fascinating city."

Carolyn Campbell
Published articles in *People, Redbook,
Ladies' Home Journal,* and *Writer's Digest*

11-30-2017
Finished ...

Tales from...
Two-Bit Street
and beyond...
Part II

Ghostly Legends from Ogden's

Historic 25th Street

Drienie Hattingh

Copyright © 2013
Drienie Hattingh and Lynda Scott
Tales from Two-Bit Street and Beyond, Part II
ISBN-13: 978-1542355667
ISBN-10: 1542355664

All rights reserved, including the right of reproduction. No part of this book may be used or reproduced in any manner whatsoever without written permission of the editors or the individual authors.

Compiled by: Drienie Hattingh
Published by Drienie Hattingh and Lynda Scott
Edited by: Precision Editing
Second Editing/Formatting by: Marley Gibson

Photography:
Cover: Drienie Hattingh
Cover Design: Dimitria Van Leeuwen
Inside: Drienie Hattingh, Patricia Bossano, Cara Kolmees, Union Station Archives

This book is a work of fiction. References to real people, events, establishments, organizations or locales are intended only to provide a sense of authenticity. All other characters, and all incidents and dialogue, are drawn from the authors' imaginations and are not to be construed as real.

Printed in the United States of America
1st Printing June 2013
Revised 2nd Printing January 2017
Printed in the United States of America
Published by Cardinal Rules Press

Cardinal Rules
PRESS

Dedication

I dedicate this book to my Mother, Ralie Naude.
She has always been supportive of me and my writing.
During her three-month visit with us in 2012 from South
Africa, she accompanied us to the Farmer's Market
every single Saturday. Her obvious pride and joy in
being with me at every book signing on those hot and
humid mornings, meant the world to me.

Here's to you, Mammie… love you always.
When I grow up, I want to be like you.

Table of Contents

Foreword

Drienie Hattingh

I love this street! This is where I live.

When we moved here and I learned all about the rich, colorful history, and explored all the historical buildings, I knew I had to write about it and encouraged others to do the same. This is how this anthology came to be.

Historic 25th Street has always been about music. In the olden days, many jazz clubs lined this street, and blues players, such as Count Basie, Duke Ellington, Dizzy Gillespie and BB King performed here. Today the clubs and coffee shops host local up-and-coming musicians, and sometimes big names roll into town too.

Ogden has hosted several presidents too. Theodore Roosevelt, Herbert Hoover and Harry Truman visited this quaint town. Eleanor Roosevelt loved the town's diversity, friendly folks and its towering mountains.

However, the person I would have loved to meet on this street in the early years would have been Ernest Hemingway who, it is said, often visited clubs on 25th Street—in disguise.

Moviemakers frequently head to Ogden for the remarkable setting it offers. TV series like *Everwood* was filmed here and even had permanent movie sets, including the white and green 'Everwood Train Station' tucked in-between the old buildings. In 1985, the Chevy Chase movie, *Fletch*, was filmed in part of downtown Ogden. More recently, the upper part of 25th Street was turned into a winter-wonderland for the TV Christmas Movie, *The Mistle-Tones* with Tia Mowrie and Tori Spelling. Locals just smile when they arrive for a shopping excursion or to dine and find the street is closed for a movie shoot, bike race, marathon or festival.

Some of the year-round events include First Friday, Arts Stroll, Winterfest, Ogden Arts Festival, Farmers Market, Worldwide on 25th, Harvestmoon Festival, Witchstock and more. The *Christmas Lighting Festival* and parade, are a must see. Millions of lights shimmer in the park dotted with Christmas Houses.

This area is now filled with great restaurants—nineteen in all—and boasts an artsy movie theater, coffee and ice cream shops, antique stores, salons, bars, bakeries, art galleries and other unique shops.

Historic 25th Street, flanked by the Ben Lomond Hotel on the east and the Union Station on the west, is steeped in history, including the colorful period between the late 1800s and the first half of the 20th century when "Junction City" was the crossroads of the west. Back then, the street was known for its brothels, opium dens, and bootlegging. Because of all the infamous history there are countless recounts of hauntings and legends.

Historic Union Station has many legends. One originated during, what Standard Examiner called, "One of the West's worst rail accidents." With all the people who died in this accident, local mortuaries were full and the Browning Theater, located in the Union Station, had to be turned into a temporary mortuary.

The present day beautifully preserved Union Station, now close to a hundred years old, was preceded by wooden structure that housed a hotel and restaurant. This 36-year-old building was destroyed by fire and burned to the ground on February 13, 1923.

Not far from the Union Station, one block up, on the corner of 25th and Lincoln Streets, is the still popular *Moore's Barber Shop*, where skilled barbers, have been shaving men's faces, and cutting their hair, since the early 1900's. Myron Fuller was one of the owners of Moore's until shortly before his death in 1921. His grandson contributed to, and authorized, the release of the story in this anthology, "Shave and a Haircut…" written by Lynda West Scott.

Across the street, from Moore's is another historical building, *Hotel Helena*, with its own secrets and legends. And, right next to it, on the corner, is the building where, in the 1940s, the infamous Rosetta Duccini Davie ran the classiest establishment of ill-repute on Two-Bit Street, known as The Rose Rooms. She was known as

Rose, the beautiful raven-haired and red-lipped woman, and the kindest soul in the roughest of towns. Ogdenites, at the time, saw her regularly, driving her fancy black Lincoln, or walking her pet ocelot up and down 25th Street, or as it was then know, Two-Bit Street.

Then, there are the tunnels beneath this historic street. Many speculate about these tunnels... do they exist or not? Many swear by it. They tell stories that were passed on through the generations of the tunnels beneath Ogden. And the evidence is there. In the basements of all the historic buildings, right from Ben Lomond Hotel, up to the Union Station, there are bricked-in entryways that were used to access the tunnels. Some say the tunnels weren't built that well, and caved in during an earthquake in 1934 and they are now closed because of the safety issues.

Another landmark... The *Broom Hotel* (now gone) that was situated on the corner of Washington Boulevard and 25th Street, right across from the City Gardens. It was known throughout the west and the pride and glory of Ogden City and the most luxurious hotel between the Mississippi River and the West Coast.

There are still some old-timers who remember this street with fondness. Some grew up on this street and are defensive about the fact that it was a terrible place. They argue that it was also a place where families worked and lived and had a good life. Such is Fred Seppi, who was so gracious to share his memories of growing up on Two-Bit Street in this anthology.

Others still hold onto the 'bad' history, even beyond Utah's border. Proof of this is when my neighbor, Dorothy Elliott visited family in Larchmont, California and had her hair done.

After hearing where Dorothy lived, the hairdresser said, "Do you know Al Capone felt Ogden was more dangerous than Chicago?"

Introduction

Stan Trollip

Two-Bit Street! What a wonderful name! It's a street with a turbulent history. Good and bad—up and down—in a town with an equally colorful past. Ogden, Utah, a town that Al Capone said was too rough for him.

Today 25th Street (its real name) is a thriving street in a prosperous town. Walking down its length, one can see glimpses of its past. A few new buildings set amongst the old. For most visitors, however, there is little to give away what happened in its past: prostitution, bootlegging, murder.

A year ago, the co-editors, Drienie Hattingh and Lynda Scott, asked local writers to submit stories, based on legends from Historic 25th Street's colorful past, and they produced an anthology of short stories titled *Tales from Two-Bit Street and Beyond ... Part I.*

The goal with that first book was to recapture the feel of Historic 25th Street through a collection of ghost stories that mirrored what happened there so many years ago. And what a success it was! The thirteen stories run the gamut of good ghosts, scary ghosts, and inexplicable happenings. People of the past popped up in the present, and people of today moved back into the past. By the end of the book, the reader is left knowing 25th Street—at least some of it. In a sense 25th Street is a fourteenth story in the book.

Now we have *Tales from Two-Bit Street and Beyond ... Part II*. It is another anthology of creepy stories—thirteen of them—that continues to build the legend of 25th Street.

Again the stories are varied in their topics, and all are thought-provoking, tapping into that part of us that is not certain whether to believe in ghosts or not.

The Last Dance is a sadly romantic story of a young woman falling in love as she is dying from leukemia. In *Shave and Haircut-Two Bits,* a man returns to Ogden after many years and has a close shave from a barber who uses a cut-throat razor. And, he learns a lot about his past. In *205 ½ 25th Street*, a man visits a building where a woman, Rose, once talked his grandmother out of having an abortion. This one-time lady of the night tries to seduce him, causing him to decide he would in future only date living women.

In *The Legend of the Union Station Fire*, the community of ghosts that inhabit the station is a playful group which results in a fire with dire consequences.

The newest addition to the TALES series is a great read from beginning to end. This time, however, Drienie had to go it alone after Lynda relocated to California. So, we have to thank Drienie for pulling together another delightful offering. I can only hope there is a Part III.

 Stanley Trollip writes with Michael Sears under the name Michael Stanley. The first three of their Detective Kubu mysteries (set in Botswana) garnered thirteen shortlist nominations for awards in the United States and the United Kingdom. *Death of the Mantis* won the Barry Award for Best Paperback Original and was shortlisted for an Edgar Award. The fourth mystery, *Deadly Harvest,* was released in April 2013.

January 1, 1945, The Ogden Standard Examiner:

"Some 50 persons died and 80 others were injured in the Sunday crash of a speeding southern Pacific mail-express and a slowly-moving passenger train both westbound on a fog-shrouded causeway near Bagley, in shallow waters of Great Salt Lake, 17 miles west of Ogden... The train had left Chicago at ten a.m. Friday, bound for San Francisco."

1. The Last Dance
Drienie Hattingh

The Browning Theater looked lovely.

Ben, Molly, myself, and other volunteers had spent that whole day decorating the ballroom in 1920s style with lots of little yellow lights adorning the four Christmas trees, one in each corner of the big dance hall. Above it all, we hung plastic globes, in all different sizes—some enormous—on strings from the wooden rafters. The result was a yellow golden glow filling the entire room.

The Leukemia Research Association was having their charity ball and dinner here tomorrow night.

I smiled. We really didn't have to do much to get this hall to look like the 1920s! No need for make-believe. It was over a hundred years old—one hundred percent authentic—from the parquet floors to the arched windows and the high-beamed ceilings.

All of the sudden, I don't know why, a terrible thought permeated my happy mood.

The Browning Theater had once been a morgue.

"So, what do you think of our handy work?" Ben said next to me and made me jump.

"Ha! Scared ya," he said as he draped his arm over my shoulders. Then he looked down into my face and frowned. "Are you cold? You're shivering." Then with concern written all over his face he asked, "Tracey, are you okay?"

I knew he was thinking I was having one of my fainting spells.

"No, Ben," I said with a smile. "I'm fine. I just remembered that this place used to be a morgue."

Molly joined us. "Oh! I just love what we did. Those light bulbs give the whole place an out-of-this-world look, but it still doesn't take away that '20s look. This must be our best job ever."

Even though I still felt spooked, I agreed. "It is lovely. I wonder how they decorated for Christmas in the olden days."

As if Molly read my earlier thoughts, she said, "Gosh, when I think of those days, I can't help but think of this place as a morgue. Remember? In the 1940s when all those people died in that train wreck, the local mortuaries were full, so they used this place as a temporary morgue? Just imagine rows of corpses lying here, right where we now stand."

Ben placed his other arm around Molly and walked us both out of the theater. "Stop being so morbid, silly woman. Let's go have dinner at the Union Grill. My treat."

***

"Sweetie, you look beautiful," Mom said softly as I walked down the stairs to where she stood in the entrance hall, waiting with her old fashioned camera—the kind you still put film in. How can she still wait for the photos to be developed, not knowing what it will look like? Mom also doesn't have a cell phone or a computer.

Dad joined us, and the old softy got tears in his eyes too as he looked at me. He gave me a huge bear hug, lifting me off my feet.

"You must enjoy the dance tonight, my darling. You always loved to dance. But promise me you'll call if you feel sick or dizzy. I'll come and get you. But if you are okay, please enjoy the evening and don't shoo the guys off, dance with them. Don't do

as you always do: show your face and then leave...
promise?"

I nodded. I knew what Dad meant. I have an
obligation to go to these functions, but I always
leave as soon as I can. Why try to meet a guy, when
there might be no time to get to know him?

I stopped asking, "Why did this happen to me?"
long ago. Leukemia, I always thought, was a
childhood disease. Well, apparently not. The
constant blood transfusions were so tedious, and I
really couldn't see the point, if I was going to die
anyway. But I did it for my parents. They wanted
me to keep on trying. My prognosis wasn't good,
but Mom and Dad were praying it would go in
remission.

After five years, it was still with me.
Nevertheless, my parents clung to their hopes of a
good outcome. Mom said she read somewhere that
80% of people with leukemia grow out of it. I
wanted to tell her I've stopped growing but didn't.
Let her hope—I'm her only child after all.

After that first awful year, I made them promise
to allow me to have a normal life as long as it was
possible. I wasn't going to spend what was left of
my life living like an invalid. I wanted to drive my
car and go on walks and visit friends. That was
when they agreed I could be a volunteer at the
Leukemia Research Association.

Ben, who was in charge of all the fundraisers, was happy to have me. I was, so to speak, his "right hand." We worked hard on this event, called "Dance Away Your Blues."

***

I loved everything about this job—the interaction with people, finding the perfect place for the events, deciding on the themes, and then decorating accordingly. And I've made really good friends too, like Ben and his wife, Molly. I've grown quite fond of them. Of course, they knew all about my illness but never talked about it, and they have always treated me like a normal person. My doctor said it would be good for me to work. He was a bit concerned about me driving and all but said I would know when it was time to stop.

Mom took pictures of me, dressed in my black flapper dress, my hair pinned down with an Alice band with a flower on it.

"You look just like Mia Farrow in that movie, *The Great Gatsby*, sweetie," Dad said.

First, Mom made me pose on the staircase alone and then with Dad, and then Dad took pictures of Mom and me. I played along, knowing they were capturing everything until the very last seconds... my last seconds.

Tomorrow, Mom would have the photos developed and then put them in the newest album, which was almost full. Next to it waited an empty one. The bookcase in the family room was entirely filled with photo albums, mostly from after the time I was diagnosed.

"Good," Mom said. "That was the last of the film." She helped me put on my coat.

It was cold and had been snowing all day.

I enjoyed the short walk to my car. I turned my face up to the sky. I loved the feeling of snowflakes on my face. It felt like wet little feathers touching me ever so lightly. I was still infatuated with snow, even at age twenty-seven.

I settled into the driver's seat and shook my head to rid myself of the dizzy spells and tiredness. At least I wasn't in any pain. The endless pills saw to that. I started the car and drove slowly down our street and stopped at the stop sign, waiting for a stream of cars on Harrison to pass.

"It's not fair," I muttered. I hadn't said this in a very long time, but I felt so hopeless. I didn't want to tell Mom and Dad, but the tiredness and dizzy spells had increased in the last month. I was so tired of life, knowing it would not get better.

I whispered, "God, please take me before I turn into a total invalid." I didn't think I would be able to live like that.

Someone honked behind me, and I saw the street was clear. I turned left on Harrison and made a right turn onto 25th Street. Far down below, through the falling snow, I could see the red letters spelling out my destination: The Ogden Union Station.

My arms felt weak where they rested on the steering wheel, and I knew, even though I intended to stay longer tonight, I wouldn't be able to. When I got to Washington Boulevard, four blocks from the station, I had to stop for the red light at the intersection. Regardless of my state of mind, I smiled at the scene in front of me.

The city park sparkled with thousands of colorful lights—in the trees and on the little Christmas houses scattered throughout the square. It was a proverbial winter wonderland; yellow lights shone from the tiny windows of the houses, and a blanket of snow covered everything lining historic 25th Street, all the way down to Union Station.

The light turned green and I moved forward, still smiling. Out of the corner of my eye, I saw a moving truck, sliding right through the red light on the snow-covered road. It was heading straight for me and my little car. In a split second, I had to make a decision. Should I accelerate? Slow down? Make a sharp turn? I went with the sharp turn.

Christmas lights swirled together in a kaleidoscope of colors. Things seemed to stretch out in slow motion. I looked up and the truck's lights burned into my eyes, but the next thing I knew I faced the opposite way and saw the truck's rear lights disappear in the distance.

"Thank God," I whispered to myself. I had made the right decision. The truck missed me by a hair. Then I smiled and leaned my head back on the seat. I marveled at human nature. Even though I had pleaded with God to take me, only minutes ago, I still did what was necessary to save myself.

Pedestrians on the sidewalk, who were previously admiring the Christmas houses, now stood looking at me with horror on their faces— obviously as shocked as I was. Not everyone looking at me had shocked expressions on their faces. Some appeared happy that I managed to miss the truck. An older woman looked at me as if deep in thought, then she lifted her hand in a greeting. Next to her, a little boy smiled and winked and waved at me with enthusiasm. A man, apparently also on his way to the fundraiser ball, dressed in 1920s clothing, smiled broadly at me, lifted his bowler hat, as if to congratulate me on my nifty move to escape the truck's onslaught. Even in my state of shock, I noticed he was extremely attractive, and his smile made my heart quiver. I watched as he turned around and disappeared into the crowd of brightly and warmly dressed people.

I closed my eyes and let out a long steady breath. I turned the car around, facing Union Station again, and drove very slowly the rest of the way. I turned left onto Wall Avenue, and then made an almost immediate right turn into the station's parking lot. I was about to get out of the car when I hesitated in disbelief. The exhausting, all-enveloping tiredness that engulfed my body earlier was gone. "Ha," I said out loud. "I guess that huge surge of adrenaline was just what I needed. I might enjoy this night after all. Who knows," I said with a quivering smile, "I might even be able to dance the blues away!"

As I walked through the doors at the Browning Theater, I gasped at the beautiful sight. Now, at night, with no light from the outside, the softly lit moon bulbs threw a warm golden glow over the dance hall. It looked so romantic.

"Good evening, ma'am."

The deep baritone behind me made me jump, and I turned around with a little yelp.

"Oh, I am sorry," the man said with an apologetic smile.

Goodness, I thought, *be still my heart! Love that accent... Chicago? And he's so handsome with his wavy brown hair and twinkling green eyes. And he looks so comfortable in his period clothes. But oh, more than anything, I thought, that smile.*

"You... you... look the part," I managed to stammer.

"Yes, I love to dress up. You are lovely," he said, still smiling at me.

I felt the heat creep into my face. "Thank you." Then I frowned and tilted my head. "You look familiar."

Even as I spoke I realized where I'd seen him before—he was the man who lifted his hat at me after my near escape barely half an hour before. "You were at... "

"Yes, that was me," he said, now with compassion.

He looked as though he wanted to say more, but I had to excuse myself because the caterers had arrived. I walked over to them to show them where the food had to go, but Molly beat me to it. I stopped in my tracks. What was Molly doing here? It was her night off. She looked upset, and I noticed Ben did too. *Oh, no!* Something must have gone wrong with the arrangements. I moved toward them but noticed the band had arrived, and I had to show them where to set up. However, Ben was with them before I could get there.

The room filled with tantalizing sounds as the musicians tuned their instruments.

Soon the guests would be here. Someone had to be at the door to greet them and show them to their assigned seats. Both Ben and Molly were busy, so I'd have to be the greeter and seat the guests!

"Anything I can do to help?" the man with the intoxicating smile asked behind me. He was so close I could feel his warm breath on my neck.

"Um... yes... I guess... will you stand at the door and welcome the guests, and then I will guide them to their seats."

"Sure thing," he said and walked to the door.

Just then I saw Ben and Molly walk over to the door, and Ben was in time to welcome the first guests, an elderly couple.

Molly guided them to their table.

The man with the smile turned around and shrugged.

His smile made my knees weak.

"Sorry," I said. "I didn't get your name."

He extended his hand. "John McKenzie. Glad to meet you, Tracey."

I placed my hand in his, enjoying the delightful tingling his warm firm grip caused.

"How do you know my name?" I asked with a frown.

"Um... your name tag?"

"Oh, yes... of course." I felt the heat creep into my face and pulled my hand from his.

The sounds of a lovely waltz from Johann Strauss filled the air.

John tilted his head slightly and smiling that heart-melting smile of his, said, "May I have this dance?"

I placed my right hand in his and the other lightly on his shoulder.

I felt a warm sensation on my back, where his other hand rested, soft but firm, as he guided me onto the already-filled dance floor. The rest of the night went by in a delightful, dazzling swirl. Never before had I danced that much. There seemed to be no end to my newfound energy. I danced every dance with John McKenzie.

I couldn't believe it when I looked at the clock and saw it was fifteen minutes to midnight. All night long, I felt like Cinderella dancing with my Prince Charming. But a shiver ran down my spine.

What's going to happen when the clock strikes twelve?

"Everyone gather around," Ben called out. "Time for the group photo. Please go to the west wall and follow the photographer's directions."

Lots of laughing couples joined us, and we all posed as we were told.

After several shots, the photographer was satisfied.

John and I stood in the back, his arm protectively around my shoulders.

This is great, I thought sarcastically, *I'm in love at last but my life might soon be over.*

The photographer asked everyone to stay put as he scanned the images on his camera. John and I, along with Ben and Molly, peeked over the photographer's shoulder as he made sure he had enough to work with. *This is not Mom's camera,* I thought with a smile.

My eyes went immediately to the right corner on the small viewfinder.

We weren't there! What in Heaven's name?

My eyes quickly went to the other corner, thinking perhaps the photo was somehow reversed. But no, we weren't in that corner either. I looked at all the photos as the photographer scanned through them... to no avail.

"What's going on?" I whispered to John.

"Tracey, I am so sorry," he said as he led me away from the others. He put his hands on my shoulders and looked into my eyes. "I know I should have told you earlier, but you were having so much fun. Every time I wanted to say something, I couldn't. I know, I was selfish, but I didn't want to spoil our evening, not yours or mine. I wanted us to have this night before..." He hesitated and looked deep into my eyes. "We are not in the picture, because we have passed on, my dear. If I'd told you that you died when the truck hit your car, we wouldn't have had tonight."

Around me, everything had gone quiet. Ben and Molly and even the musicians and caterers were gone. A sudden feeling of understanding filled me and unexplained peace and happiness settled over me. I smiled up into John's handsome face.

"I'm glad you didn't tell me, John."

His arms went around me, and I rested my head against his chest. I thought of how I asked God to not let me become an invalid. If I couldn't go on my favorite walks next to the beautiful Ogden River or on trails in the foothills of the Wasatch Mountains or dance, like I danced tonight, I did not want to live. I now knew he gave me my wish on this lovely snowy night. He did it so beautifully. He gave me a magical night where I danced like I never danced before. I'm not tired anymore; I'm whole again.

"Who are you?" I whispered against John's shoulder.

"I died in the train accident in 1945. They brought me here, to the Browning Theater, with the other victims. I was on my way to San Francisco to start a new life. I got stuck here, tied to this building. I could never feel at peace, not until tonight."

I looked up at him, adoring his lovely green eyes.

"The moment I saw you, my darling," he whispered, "after your accident, I fell in love and knew my time in limbo was over."

With our arms wrapped around each other, we danced the last dance of the evening to music only we could hear.

2. Shave and a Haircut-Two Bits

Lynda West Scott

I'd been thinking of visiting my mother for a while and since my wife was away for the day, it seemed like a good time. I used to visit Mother every day, but now I only managed once in two or three years. Don't get me wrong, I'm still a loving son; it's just looking at the mausoleum door with her name on it isn't quite the same as hearing her say "Oh, Jack!" in the disgusted way the mother of an only spoiled child can. Having my dad's sense of humor and teasing her a lot also affected her tone.

My mother was a perfect example of the saying: "Be careful what you wish for." She and my dad had long since given up hope of having a child when I surprised them when Mother was in her forties. I must have been a challenge for her, as the "Oh, Jack!" goes back as far as I can remember. I'd hear those words and start laughing, which made her angry and she'd say, "Shut up, Jack!" making me laugh all the harder. It was disrespectful to laugh, but the look on her face and the way she said it really struck me as funny. It might come as a surprise to those who witnessed this, but we loved each other dearly, and I miss her every day.

I drove up to Ogden from Salt Lake on what we called "the Mountain Road," or Highway 89. It used to be a small two-lane road with fruit trees and fruit sellers lining the street; now it's more like a freeway with houses everywhere and very few fruit trees remaining.

When I reached the cemetery on 36th Street, it took me a few minutes to find my mother's and father's vaults. The afternoon sun glinted off Myrtle's plate in contrast to the dullness of Charlie's thirty-year-older plate. I spoke a few words to them—after making sure no one could hear me—and patted both plates before I left.

For old time's sake, I decided to check out our house near 7th North and Washington where we lived until Dad got transferred to Salt Lake City when I was seven. That bungalow house and another one just like it sat near the entrance to what is now some kind of trade school. There was only one house there now and, to be honest, I can't remember if ours was closer to the driveway to the school or not. I wanted to think ours was the one torn down, because looking at the dinginess of this one made me sad.

On the way home, I decided to check out 25th Street. The last time I drove Mother down there, her "tsk, tsk, tsk" got louder each block.

"Nothing but bars and winos here now," she grumbled. "Back when I was a girl, there were all kinds of stores: hardware, grocery, clothing, Zions Mercantile, livery stables, restaurants, banks, trolley cars, and crowds of people on the streets. There were four or five barber shops besides Dad's, but his was the largest. My sisters and I loved going to town on the trolley with Mother to visit Dad and shop, or watch people. Dad always made sure he had three sticks of candy—one for each of us girls. Sometimes, Mother would let us walk down to Union Station—not the new one," she said, pointing to the depot, "and watch passengers arriving or departing. I felt sad when the old station burned down. We came to watch the fire; I think everyone in Ogden did. It lit up the whole sky.

"My father died in 1921 before the Depression hit and the street started declining. I'm glad he didn't live to see it." Mother seemed down and didn't talk much on the way home, as if we had left a funeral for one of her best friends. I tried to tease her but couldn't get an "Oh, Jack!" out of her to save me.

Now, as I turned off Washington onto 25th Street, a nice park surrounded the city building where the jail used to be. It always gave me the willies when I was a kid when we stopped at the bank across the street. Maybe a babysitter told me she'd drop me off there if I didn't behave; I can't remember, but I was scared of it.

The street sported more stores and fewer bars, though some nutty business owner displayed window-sized legal documents and signs about the Ogden mayor.

Near the corner of Lincoln and 25th Street, I found a parking place and walked toward a barber shop. Mother told me this was her father's shop, but no one seemed to be sure about that. The red, white, and blue barber's pole rotated, spinning the diagonal stripes. I was surprised to see the sign operating on a Monday, especially since the shop looked dark. I moved closer to the front door, but couldn't see much for the glare. I cupped my hands around my eyes and leaned against the glass.

"Shit!" I thought—or perhaps screamed—when two eyes materialized in front of mine. I stepped back quickly, and it was all I could do not to run, but then I rationalized it was probably just the reflection of my eyes in the window. After a moment, I moved closer to the door. I still couldn't see in with the glare, but I had to find out if it was a reflection.

My heart about stopped and I jumped when I heard the door creak. I watched it open, slowly, slowly. I commanded my feet to run, but a part of me felt too fascinated to move. When I looked up to where I expected to see eyes, I did. But I also saw a face, and a whole body below it.

"Hi there, young man," said the door-opener.

When the shock wore off, I smiled at the thought of a man in his fifties or sixties calling me young. Hell, I had to be ten or fifteen years older than him.

"Ah... hi," I replied, as if I'd just learned to talk. "I thought you were closed. Sorry for window-peeping."

"We're closed on Mondays, but I came in to sharpen my blades. It's nice and quiet in here for a change." He grinned. "Why don't you come in for a shave and I'll test my sharpening skills?"

When he said "shave," my hand automatically reached up to my face and I felt the stubble I'd decided not to bother with this morning. Retirement sometimes makes me lazy.

"No. It's your day off. I just wanted to look around. I heard my grandfather used to own this barber shop."

"No fooling?" he asked. "What was his name?"

"Myron Fuller," I said, and then quickly explained, "but I never met him. He died eleven years before I was born."

"Oh, too bad. He was a nice man."

"You knew him?" I asked, astonished. How could this man who looked younger than me have known my grandfather?

"Well, I've heard a lot about him," he said. "Why don't you come in, and I'll tell you about him while I give you a shave?"

I was sitting in the barber's chair before I realized I'd moved.

"I'll heat up a towel and give you the works," he said as he moved around placing a towel in a heater, and an old-fashioned shaving cup and a brush and straight razor with ivory handles on a shelf near my chair. *Interesting*, I thought. They must be old since ivory isn't used anymore.

He flicked the razor over the leather strop several times and tested the blade. I felt confused.

Did he say he had already sharpened his razors, or that he was going to? I must have interrupted him before he finished.

The barber lowered the seat back and made sure I was comfy before he retrieved the hot towel. He wrapped my entire face except for my nose, and I pictured myself looking like someone in an old movie. I didn't know if I liked the idea of my face being wrapped up like a mummy and not being able to see. I reached a hand up to lift one side a bit to give me some peeking ability, but he cautioned me to keep the wrap tight for the best effect.

"Relax and enjoy it for a few minutes. Let it soften your beard. I'll wake you if you start to snore," he quipped.

The hot towel created a cozy cocoon, and I did begin to relax; I might even have dozed because I'd become accustomed to an afternoon nap. I think I jolted when he began to speak.

"Your grandpa ran quite a shop," he said. "Oh. Did I wake you? You weren't even snoring." He began uncoiling the hot towel.

"Tell that to my wife."

He laughed and then continued talking about Grandpa Fuller. "Seven other barbers besides him, and busy most of the time. He supported a wife and three daughters on his earnings."

While he stirred the soap in the shaving mug and lathered it on my face, he provided me with interesting tidbits about my grandfather, Ogden, and Two-Bit Street, as he called it.

With the quickness of a cat, he shaved away the soapy foam and whiskers, all the while talking and lifting my chin, or turning my cheek. The razor in his hand was like a baton to an orchestra leader, whipping around with grace and ease. In minutes, he had wiped away the excess soap, rubbed a soothing lotion on my face and whipped off the cape.

"How's that feel? Smooth as a baby's bottom?" He chuckled.

It did. I'd never had a shave like that and it made me wonder what it would have been like to know my grandfather and to have been shaved by him.

"You're right there. Smoothest shave I've ever had. How much do I owe you?"

"Two bits."

"Two bits?" I said. "That's only a quarter. Seriously, what do you charge?"

"No. Two-bits, it is." He played with the end of his wide mustache as he spoke.

"Well, I'll just have to give you a generous tip then," I said.

After some argument, he ended up taking a few dollars, and we both seemed disappointed—he because I paid too much, and me because I didn't pay enough.

"Hope to see you around sometime, young man," he said as he walked me to the door.

I laughed and said, "Maybe so, old-timer."

The drive home found me deep in thought about the barber and my grandfather—an interesting pair.

Several months later, I decided to check out the barber shop again. I drove by the Ben Lomond Hotel. It didn't seem much different, but looked better than the last time I brought Mother up. Then I saw Peery's Egyptian Theater. What a change. It looked almost new. Memories of cartoon shows and movies with my older cousins flooded back—the giggles, the popcorn, being scared in some of the shows, but not wanting anyone to know.

I continued down to 23rd Street, where I remembered a shopping mall was now a big movie theater and a few restaurants and businesses. North of the theater was a large building called the Solomon Center, which advertised indoor parachuting. Amazing! Not that I ever wanted to skydive—indoors or out.

On Wall Avenue, I stopped at Union Station and walked around inside. Mother and I took the passenger train from Salt Lake many times to visit her family in Ogden and we walked through this very lobby. The ceiling seemed as high as it had when I was a kid, but there weren't many benches now. Without the trains, there was no need for them. A model train ran through a display in a window in the hallway, and through an open door, I saw some old cars in a large room. I didn't want to take time to tour, but I made a note to see the Browning Gun Museum the next time I came up.

The Front Runner train was parked north of the old depot. It looked like something out of our Flash Gordon comics, all sleek and bright—nothing like the old black trains. I decided to try it when I came to visit the museum.

By this time, I realized it was Monday and I had no hope of seeing the barber again, but I walked up the street anyway. The barber pole spun around, but the shop looked dark. I peeked in again and didn't see anyone at first, but almost as if he materialized from nothing, I saw him. He smiled and walked to the door and unlocked it.

"Come in, come in. I'm glad to see you. Come for another shave?" His smile scrunched up his wide gray mustache.

"I'm surprised you're here again on a Monday."

"Oh, I'm here a lot of the time," he said, his eyes twinkling.

I wasn't sure what he meant by that, but I assumed it meant being out of his wife's hair.

"How about another shave?" he asked, and then seeming to notice my clean-shaven face, he said, "Or I could give you a bit of a trim. Your hair isn't long, but I'll have you looking great."

He turned the chair toward me and had me wrapped in a cape before my bum hit the seat.

"The old comb-over, I see," he laughed. "Not much left to cut on top—just like me. I'll trim your neck and ears."

After he finished, his magic fingers began massaging my head and neck. It was heaven, and I dozed again.

When I roused myself a bit, I asked, "Do you live around here?"

"Not too far away. We're near 26th and Fowler. Nice home, but a bit too large now that the girls are married. Still, it's home and I expect we'll stay there until we're too old to take care of ourselves, or until I die." He said this last part with an uncommon, downhearted look that alarmed me.

"Are you sick?" I asked before I remembered my manners. "I'm sorry. It's none of my business."

"No, it's okay. I've had a bit of heartburn and pain, but I'm fine. Say," he said as if to change the subject, "did you ever wonder how the barber pole came about? I heard back in the days when barbers were also blood-letters and tooth-pullers, red represented blood and white the bandages. Blue was perhaps for the vein color. The ball on top originally was a blood-collecting bowl."

I found this interesting, but I couldn't quite put away his heartburn statement. He seemed to guess I would turn the topic back to that because he pulled out his pocket watch and said, "Oh, look at the time. I must be off, but please come again. There's so much more I'd love to tell you about your grandfather."

I did go back, time after time, but always on a Monday. "It's the best day for me," he'd said. I toured the museums at Union Station, bought coffee at Grounds for Coffee, and sweet rolls for my wife at a bakery. I ate a doughnut now and again—well, every time. I also learned a lot from the barber about my grandfather and the town back in the late 1800s and into the early 1920s. One day he said, "You know Ogden, or as it used to be called, Junction City, had its seedy side, too."

This surprised me after the glowing description my mother painted of the town, but she probably never knew about that, or didn't want me to think of her hometown that way.

"What do you mean?" I asked. "I noticed there were a lot of bars here years ago."

"Oh, that was later, but when the railroad moved here, prostitution, gambling, and drugs followed it from Corrine. We—I mean the businesses—operated during the day time, but at night the rowdiness came out. 'Good people' didn't come down here at night—or most of them, anyway," he said with a chuckle.

"Well, that's something Mother never told me," I said, and we both laughed.

One day I couldn't make it on a Monday and went up on Tuesday. A red Cadillac was parked at the curb on the Lincoln side of the corner. I noticed because my wife is fond of red Cadillacs, and she has one parked in the carport at home. The shop bustled with activity, but it seemed different—more modern somehow. I brushed it off to the brighter lighting and the attractive women working there. I talked with the owner, Mr. Moore, for a few minutes while he cut a man's hair with clippers and a comb. He was friendly. I asked about the other barber—I felt surprised I still didn't know his name—but Mr. Moore didn't know who I was talking about. I tried describing him, and then Mr. Moore's face lit up.

"Did he have a wide mustache?" he asked. "Younger fellow, in his fifties or so, balding?"

"Yeah," I said, glad he knew who I meant.

"That must be Myron Fuller. It's rumored he comes around here a bit."

Chills ran up my spine and all the hairs on my arms and the back of my neck stood on end. *Myron Fuller. My grandfather!*

"Hey, you all right?" asked Mr. Moore. "You look like you just saw a ghost."

"Yeah. I think I did," I said and walked out the door.

3. Gibson Girl

Dimitria Van Leeuwen

March 13, 1934, Deseret News:
"Yesterday, when the earth shook in the Rocky Mountain Region the works of man came to a sudden halt."

J enna liked the view from the second story windows, which faced out across 25th Street. The old building inspired her with its red bricks, their corners softened with age, and the dusty hardwood floors scratched with decades of use. It was a perfect place to record the band's CD.

She caught a glimpse of her reflection in the window: wide smile, soft brown hair, hands on her hips in a confident gesture. Turning, she moved to open the black case on a chair in the corner, and gently lifted her old guitar out.

The battered case really should be replaced—one latch was missing and the velvet inside was beginning to peel away—but it had belonged to her great-grandfather whom she had never met.

He had been a mystery. He had raised his daughter, Jenna's grandma, all on his own. Who her mother was, no one in the family ever knew, and he wouldn't speak of her.

When Jenna was ten years old, she found the guitar in her grandma's dusty attic. She had been teaching herself to play and write songs ever since.

Jenna turned on the new pick-up inside the guitar, and then flipped the power switch on the small amplifier. As a test, she set up one track that would record both her voice and guitar. She adjusted the microphones, and then clicked the "record" button on the computer screen.

As she began to play, the guitar case hit the floor behind her. Startled, she frowned. She was certain it had been resting securely on the chair. She resumed playing, her fingers plucking a soft, melancholy song, the minor chords rising and falling.

She closed her eyes as she sang. She felt her voice reverberate throughout the room. A stillness and warmth and a gentle sadness settled over her heart while her fingers danced over the strings. And she felt... not alone. The feeling of being adored and watched over that she'd experienced as a young girl came back to her, tinged with an inexplicable sorrow. Her voice filled with the emotion of it.

When she finished, she sat in the quiet holding the guitar. After a time, she went to the computer and clicked "stop." She scrolled back to the beginning of the track and pushed play. The notes came out clear and lovely. The acoustics here were truly perfect for an old-timey sound. She skimmed the recording, making mental notes of things she'd like to try.

As the song neared its end, she froze, chills running up her arms. She could hear another voice. Her heart pounded as she rewound and listened to the track again. On the last chorus, it was unmistakable; someone sang along with her in a sweet harmony.

Jenna played it back later that night for her band mates, Austin and Mason.

"I know what this is," Austin, the mandolin player, said. "It's called an EVP, Electronic Voice Phenomenon. They use it on ghost hunting shows." He grinned knowingly. "There's a spirit here."

The band's bass player, Mason, seemed unmoved.

"Wait, what's this?" Austin said.

Near the beginning of the recording, they heard a thump.

"My guitar case fell off the chair," Jenna explained.

"But right before... " Austin played it again. "Here, right before you hear it fall."

They all held their breath and listened, and this time heard a whispery voice.

"It sounds like a woman."

"What is she saying... ?"

"*You're here...* " Jenna and Mason said in unison, and looked at each other with wide eyes.

***

At home, early the next morning, Jenna decided to go up into the attic. Her grandmother, Daisy, was still sleeping so she walked up the steep, narrow stairs quietly.

Sunlight filtered in through the dust-covered windows. The big room was warm and inviting; the slanted beams overhead glowed red-gold in the morning sun. She remembered an imaginary friend she had played with as a little girl. He was tall and skinny and wore a cowboy hat. He was the one who showed her the old guitar tucked away in the corner.

She stopped at a trunk that held only books. As she looked inside, she saw a small, untitled leather volume. She carefully opened it and read the hand written first page.

John Edgar Reed, 1933.

"John Reed?" She said out loud and then whispered, "Wait—this is my great-grandfather's diary."

She held the beautifully bound book in her hands; it fell open to where several pages had been torn out.

The last entry was dated June 29, 1933

Good day today. I'm dog-tired. I'll sleep well which is good because I leave first thing in the morning to get the sheep up to Ogden. Even with this damned Depression on, the stockyards will be plenty busy. The new Stock Exchange building makes things easier to transact the business end of things. There's even a telegraph office there so I can send word back to the ranch if I need to stay in town longer.

What's in those missing pages? She wondered. Then Jenna's heart pounded when her eyes fell on the date again. Grandma Daisy had been born in March of 1934.

She closed the diary and held it close to her as she ran down the treacherous little steps, from the attic to the kitchen, to show her grandmother. But the house was quiet, and no one answered her call.

On the fridge was a note, "Gone shopping."

Jenna felt restless, excited over her discovery. Her eyes fell on her guitar, and she grabbed it with one hand, the diary in the other, and headed out the door.

She pulled into a parking spot in front of the three-story building on 25th street. The Helena had been a hotel a long time ago but changed hands several times over the years.

She unlocked the front door and made her way to the second floor. When she entered the room, she found that the strong, unexpected sensation of being adored enveloped her again, as it had the day before.

She paused to let the feeling settle over her, then set the diary on a chair, and leaned her guitar in its case against the wall. As Jenna walked over to set up the microphone, a *thump* and a jangle of strings made her turn to see the guitar had fallen to the floor.

"Oh, no!" She rushed back to open the case to see if the guitar was all right. It felt warm to the touch. When she lifted it out, the end of a string snagged on the velvet lining and tore it free from the case. She frowned and untangled the string, then checked the guitar for damage. It seemed fine. She turned her attention to the fabric hanging in the case and noticed something tucked in behind the lining.

Pulling the velvet back just a bit more, she saw something hidden in there. She gently pulled it out and stared at the aged paper. Her heart raced; the paper looked familiar, just like the pages in the diary she discovered that morning. A smaller piece fell into her lap. It was an old photograph of a woman in her late twenties. Jenna paused a moment to study the face in the picture. She seemed so familiar, even with her stylized make-up and hair from what looked like the 1930s. Then she reached for the diary and opened it to the spot where pages had been torn out. The pages she found in the guitar case fit perfectly.

She sank to the floor, her back against the wall, and began to read.

Saturday, July 1, 1933

I got a better price today for the sheep than I'd expected, and I took a walk on 25th street to buy some supplies. Turning a corner I walked right past what was known, infamously, as Electric Alley. I heard a sharp whistle and as I glanced down the alley, I couldn't believe what I saw. A row of female torsos leaned out of Dutch doors, like horses in a stable. There were women, some wearing only their underthings, sitting on the little steps in the sunshine. A couple of them actually sat in their windowsills—skirts up so high you could see where their stockings were attached...

I could see there were some pretty ones in the lot, and I'm a man who can be roped in by the charms of a feminine creature, but I figured I'd best not get into that bit of trouble. I just tipped my hat to them and kept walking.

I no sooner passed the alley, shaking my head in wonder, than a gust of wind blew up the street and carried off the hat of a young woman ahead of me. She reached up to catch it but was too late, and it sailed into the branches of the tree nearest me. She was so pretty with her short dark curls flying free that my wits took temporary leave to enjoy the sight. I just stood there and smiled until she asked was I gonna help her or just stand there gawking? I reached up to the branch for her hat and unfastened it. When I returned it to her, I was rewarded with a most gracious smile.

She carefully re-pinned the small hat onto her lovely curls and I noticed her dainty white gloves. I'll be damned if I can say why but something about the blue flowers on her dress and her blue eyes— well, I decided right then and there that I would make the permanent acquaintance of this little gal.

I tipped my hat to her and said I hoped her finery hadn't been damaged. She replied no, it was just fine, thank you. I asked her was she in need of the retrieval of any other objects out of her reach?

At this she raised an indignant eyebrow and inquired whether I might be in need of a sock in the nose?

Well, this made me laugh right out loud and I apologized, and asked if by way of making amends I might be allowed to buy her a soda?

She paused for a long moment. I believe she was meaning to send me on my way, but she gave me a long hard look right in the eye, then a funny little smile and said that'd be swell.

On the walk to the corner of 25th and Washington Street, we made our introductions. She was Sylvia Lawson, born in Boston. When I asked her what brought her to Junction City, she only told me, "The train."

We hadn't time for further personal enlightening before we reached The Little Sweet Shop. The place lived up to its name, just one room filled with all manner of hard candies, bonbons, and boxes of chocolates. We sat on stools at the counter near the soda fountain, and she made wisecracks about movie stars and local politicians until we howled with laughter, drawing an outright disgusted look from a woman with a young boy at the counter. Sylvie shrugged and daintily pulled her gold compact from her little handbag and began to apply her siren-red lipstick.

She asked if I was a cowboy as she twisted a little on her bar stool, her little feet perched on the top rung. A good deal of ankle showed below the ruffle of her skirt, shimmering from the fine stockings she wore.

I assured her I wasn't a cowboy but a movie star in disguise so I wouldn't have to sign any autographs. I told her I was heading back home to Hollywood to give Clark Gable a little vacation.

She dug into her purse for a small silver case with pearl inlay. She flipped it open and delicately lifted out a rolled cigarette.

I found the matches I use for my pipe and lit her cigarette, smiling at her.

She pressed the cigarette between her lips, tilted her head back to exhale, and remarked it was getting late and she needed to get going.

I extracted a promise from her to meet the next day, then I found this room at the Hotel Helena on the second floor overlooking 25th Street and I've been writing all evening. My life will never be the same after today and neither will hers.

Sunday, July 2, 1933
This morning, before I met Sylvie, I looked in a shop window and saw the prettiest little guitar in an open case lined with maroon velvet. It had an ebony finish and a fire-striped tortoise pick-guard. It cost me 35.00, but I had it in mind it would help me woo

Sylvie so it seemed money well spent.

She was late. As I waited for her, my gut felt hollow when I thought she wouldn't meet me. Then I saw her petite figure coming around the corner, the smile wide on her lovely face.

We had an early dinner at the Union Station and planned to see a movie afterward. We talked and laughed with locals and travelers waiting for the next train. Sylvie seemed to be fairly well known in this part of town.

Sylvie excused herself to go and powder her nose, and I went to pay the bill. The bartender shook his head like he might just pity me.

I asked him why he had an ornery look. He raised his eyebrows as he told me that I hadn't been around much and plum didn't know what I'd gotten myself into.

Well, that raised my hackles, and I asked what he meant. He looked up at me and told me in a low, mean tone that Sylvie was one of those girls from Electric Alley.

I looked right back at him and said well maybe she was, but not for long.

I felt a gentle hand on my shoulder and Sylvie told me we should get out of that dump.

All the way up 25th street, we didn't speak. As we rounded the corner on Washington, she took my hand, and together we walked to the magnificent

Peery's Egyptian Theater. I don't remember much of the movie. Clark Gable and Claudette Colbert were the stars, and it seemed to have a happy ending, but mostly I remember Sylvie's hand in mine.

Afterward, she said goodnight to me in front of my hotel. She wouldn't let me walk her home. I asked her to spend tomorrow with me, just one more day.

And she said yes! I can't even think of sleep. I have plans to make.

Monday, July 3, 1933

I was up early, and made my first stop at John S. Lewis' shop on Washington. I found what I was looking for almost immediately.

I met Sylvie in front the Ben Lomond Hotel, where we had a nice lunch, laughing and talking.

When we were finished, I pulled a small, velvet-covered box from my pocket. I opened the top, and a diamond ring gleamed in the soft light of the chandeliers. I got right down on one knee and looked into her pretty blue eyes. She looked horrified.

"Sylvia, darling... "

"I'm sorry," she whispered and pushed back from the table, nearly running from the restaurant.

I rushed after her, calling her name until she slowed to a stop and stood staring at the ground.

I told her I was sorry I sprang it on her like that and I probably should have waited, but she said nothing.

We walked again, not talking, and stopped in front of my hotel. She took my hand, "Mind if I come up?" she asked softly. I opened the door for her and, ignoring the smirk of the desk clerk, she walked with me to my room.

I'm writing this now by the light of a candle on the dresser. I can look over and see her exquisite form under the quilt, asleep, angelic. This is the woman I will marry.

Tuesday, July 4, 1933
In the morning, we lay for a long while in that creaky little bed and held onto each other. Finally I reached over and grabbed my new guitar announcing I was about to serenade her. I sang to her about cowboys and movie stars which made her laugh.

I still thought I could change her mind but should have known better.

Jenna took a deep breath. She felt a presence as if someone was reading along with her.

Saturday, March 10, 1934
I can't forget her. I've sent her many letters, with no reply. I'm going to Ogden in the morning.

This time, I'll find her and bring her home with me.

The next page was dated almost three weeks later. It read:

The events I record next are as correct and true as my broken heart can remember them. I arrived on March 11, Sunday morning, and went to Electric Alley. It was early, and a rare sunny day in March. A couple of the girls were up, sweeping their small steps or smoking cigarettes in the morning sun. I approached one of them and asked if she could tell me where Sylvie was. She nodded to a little house tucked away in the middle of the block.

The door was open, and Sylvie sat on a chair in a shaft of sunlight that had found its way into the house. She was knitting—pale yellow yarn gathered on her lap. When she looked up, her face flushed a pretty pink. Taking a breath, she set her yarn aside and stood awkwardly, her chin up, hand on her hip, letting me have a good look at her. She was pregnant. Pretty far along, too, it seemed to me. My heart melted and I wanted to hold her, to protect her and take care of her. I felt like I'd fight off a pack of wolves with my bare hands to keep her safe.

"Yes, Cowboy, this is your doing."

I took her in my arms and told her everything would be all right now. I wasn't going anywhere without her ever again.

She gathered a few things and we walked across the street, back to the Helena. I signed us in as Mr. and Mrs. Reed. In my heart, that was fact.

There had never been anyone else since I rescued her little hat from that tree.

We sat together on the embroidered coverlet, and I told her we would be married immediately. I still had the ring.

"All right, Cowboy, you win," she smiled.

I was overjoyed.

The next morning, March 12, we awoke a couple of minutes after eight o'clock to the sounds of a bustling 25th Street outside our window. I smiled down at her pretty face just as we felt the first of the tremors. A low rumble began slowly then increased. The porcelain pitcher shook, knocking into its basin, then crashed to the floor. We heard screams coming from the street and cracking sounds. I thought this was the end and then, for almost a minute, everything was silent. I turned to Sylvie and saw her eyes grow wide. She clutched the sheet and grimaced in pain. "You might want to fetch the doctor, Jack."

The tremors began again. The building shook like Hell itself but it didn't come down around our ears like I feared it might. The mirror shuddered itself right off the dresser and smashed onto the

57

floor but everything else stayed more or less put. And, in the middle of that earthquake, with just the two of us to get through it, our baby girl was born.

Afterward, as I gently placed her in Sylvie's arms, I realized the earth had become quiet again. Sylvie was so very pale, but she smiled tiredly. She squeezed my hand. "I think I still need the doctor, Cowboy."

This worried me. I didn't want to leave her side, but I kissed her forehead and said I'd be fast. But the doctor was hard to track down. I eventually found him at the train station helping with injuries from the quake.

The baby was crying, but Sylvie was quiet when we arrived. The doctor immediately checked her pulse. He turned to me, and the moment froze in time. With sadness in his eyes, he told me my wife had died. He lifted my daughter from her mother's arms and placed her in mine.

The air around Jenna seemed to buzz. A warm, slightly electric sensation began at the back of her arms, on her scalp, and then through her entire body. There was a wave of feeling, a love and a quiet joy so intense her eyes filled with tears and she let out a sob.

The room seemed edged with light. Jenna didn't speak but she knew in her heart Sylvie was rejoicing. This was why she had waited, earthbound. She had wanted Jenna, and her grandmother, to know all that transpired. She was free of the building and going to join Jack.

Then, with the sound of a guitar string vibrating, Jenna felt a rush as the bright energy filling the room seemed to rise through the ceiling. She stood, tears still in her eyes, a feeling of deep love surrounding her.

She reached for the guitar, which felt warm to the touch, and held it to her.

4. Joan

Michele McKinnon

Joan Taylor stood up straight in the middle of the large entry hall and stretched, wincing with pain as she slowly bent over again to finish mopping the seemingly endless floor. Every muscle in her body ached. She usually took great pride in making everything shine, but tonight it felt like she had been cleaning for an eternity, and her head throbbed. She heard the clatter of the other members of the cleaning crew off in other parts of the building. It was almost time for the short break they allowed themselves halfway through their routine.

She was a common cleaning woman at 73 years old—too old for such work. But no one could ever say she ran away from hard work. Every time her sons and their families came to visit her, they tried to talk her into retiring. Joan believed a person should work as long as they could. Add their contribution to society, even if it was cleaning a bank. She was sure the bank president and the other people who worked there appreciated having such a beautiful, clean building every morning. But she decided there was a limit to the work she could do now, and her family had finally talked her into retiring.

"Hey Joan," Angie, the youngest girl on the crew came over and took Joan's mop and set it aside.

"Come on, sweetie, you look like you could use a break, and I brought donuts for everybody tonight to celebrate. It's Andy's and my one year anniversary today."

"Oh, Angie, I'm sorry you have to be here," Joan said, easing herself into a chair in the bank's conference room. "You should be celebrating with Andy."

"Don't worry, Joan, we will definitely celebrate when I get done here tonight," said Angie, grinning. "That guy of mine is a keeper. He has dinner and dancing all planned out for us."

The other people trooped in, laughing and talking, but Joan leaned her head back against the chair and closed her eyes. She remembered her "guy" so vividly; it could have been yesterday she kissed him goodbye for the last time, instead of seventeen long years ago.

She had married Daniel MacDonald, her childhood sweetheart, when she was eighteen—a mere child— and he was twenty-one. Daniel had been the love of her life. They met when Daniel's family moved onto the farm next to Joan's family farm. She was ten then and didn't much like boys. Daniel was sort of a maverick—a rough and tumble boy.

At first, Joan thought he was a show-off. She tried to ignore his antics, but he was so friendly. He teased her, but often carried her books home from school. He even helped with her chores if he got his done first.

They began to date just before Daniel graduated from high school. He asked her to his Senior Prom, and Joan felt awkward at first. They had been friends for so long, and she felt so young and silly next to this tall, handsome young man. But when Daniel led her onto the dance floor and his arm encircled her waist, she felt shivers run up and down her back. She gazed into his liquid brown eyes and could hardly speak. He grinned at her and swept her away in a whirlwind of dancing. Joan lost track of time and of the people around them. Before she knew it, the prom ended, and they were on their way to dinner with a group of friends. It was a special treat. They went to the beautiful Broom hotel on 25th Street in downtown Ogden. They all sat at a table overlooking the moonlit mountains to the east. Joan and Daniel kept stealing glances at each other.

After that night, they fell back into their friendship, but it was different somehow, not as easy and teasing. When Daniel held her hand sometimes on the way home from school, she felt her face turn red and her whole hand and arm got tingly. He was always respectful—never even tried to kiss her.

"Are you okay?" Angie said, sitting down next to Joan. "I brought you a cream soda. I know how much you like it. It might perk you up a bit. In fact, why don't you go home and I'll do your part of the cleaning? You've helped me out plenty of times."

Joan rallied and sat up straight. "You won't do any such thing, young lady. You have a handsome young husband waiting at home for you. I'm fine, just a bit tired, and I was thinking about my husband. Do you know we came here for dinner on our first date and spent our wedding night here?"

Angie's jaw dropped. "Please tell me it's not true. You didn't really spend your wedding night stuck in a bank."

Joan laughed and sipped at her drink. "No, dear. This has only been a bank since 1960. We were married in the fall of 1918, and this was the most beautiful and luxurious hotel between Omaha and San Francisco. The bay windows on the east and south side were amazing. We had a room facing the east, so we could look out at the mountains."

"Wow, I can't believe there was such an upscale hotel, right here." Angie sighed. "I wish they hadn't torn it down. I'd love to bring Andy to a place like that. But hey, tell me about your guy, Joan. You never talk much about him."

Joan leaned back and smiled. "Oh, he was wonderful. But there was a time when I wasn't sure we would actually have a future. His name was Daniel, and right after he graduated from high school, he left to work for the summer on his uncle's ranch in Montana. I was crushed. We had only gone on one official date—the dinner date after his prom to the hotel—but I knew he was something special. And then, the very week he came home, our bishop went to Daniel's father, Glen, and said, "Glen, you have two sons of an age to go on mission. Which one are you gonna send?" And since Daniel was the oldest and had some problems with his feet—flat feet, I think they called it, and he couldn't serve in the army, the bishop got him.

When Daniel told me, I ran all the way home, and threw myself on the bed and cried myself to sleep."

"Please tell me more; we have a few more minutes before we have to finish cleaning." Angie said, planting her elbow on the table with her chin in her hand. "I'm fascinated."

Joan reached for a doughnut. "Daniel left the next week for a two-year mission to Georgia. We didn't have time to talk much the week before he left. Daniel was so busy, and I felt abandoned. I knew he was doing the right thing, but I was young, and I loved him so much. It felt like two years was an eternity, and I would never see him again.

"Of course, on the day Daniel left, I was there to see him off. He took the train from the Union Station to Salt Lake City and then on to Georgia. There were so many people there to see him off, but just before he got on the train, he pulled me aside. We stood on the platform with the engine hissing steam all around us. He kissed my cheek and, smiling at me, said, 'Remember to save some chores for me, Joan. And remember to write, at least once a week.'

"Then he said something that made me blush right down to the roots of my hair. 'I'm sorry we didn't get to talk much this week, but in truth, I was avoiding you because I knew if I talked to you, I wouldn't have the courage to leave.' And then he looked deep into my eyes and said, 'Do you know that your name means 'gift from God'? You are my gift from God, Joan Taylor, and I'll love you forever. Please wait for me.' Then the train left and he was gone."

"Oh, Joan, that is the most romantic thing I have ever heard! Andy is romantic, but your Daniel tops it all. He must have been an amazing guy. Did you get married as soon as he got home, and did you really spend your wedding night here?" Angie giggled.

Joan laughed too, but it hurt her head. "Yes, I think I cried for whole week after he left, but we wrote all during Daniel's mission. We shared our experiences, our trials, and triumphs. Two years really wasn't an eternity, and it gave me time to graduate from high school and grow up a bit. I actually worked right here in the Broom Hotel cleaning at night and in the summer. I had a tiny nest egg saved to start us out. We married that fall, and I've never regretted a moment of our life together. Our three boys came along in due time, and Daniel and I were so proud of them. They went to college, married, and have families. In fact, they all came over for Christmas this year. Oh my, we had such a house full. I wish Daniel could have been there to see how our family has grown." Joan sighed and leaned back in the chair again.

"You know, we have seven grandchildren now. And the boys have finally talked me into retiring. They have been badgering me for the last five years to retire, but I really do like my job. They promised I won't be lonesome, and I can help out with the grandchildren a little more if I'm not working. I was going to wait and tell everyone here next week, but I want you to know now."

Angie gave her a hug and brushed away a tear.

"Thank you so much for sharing, Joan. I will miss you so much." Then she laughed. "I'll remember your stories of this wonderful place to help keep the ghosts away. Sometimes when I'm off alone cleaning, I sort of feel like someone is watching me. It sounds creepy, but it really isn't. I'm beginning to see why you have worked here so long. It must help you feel closer to Daniel."

"I think the ghosts here are friendly ones," Joan said, getting stiffly to her feet. "But they sure don't help with the cleaning." She smiled as she picked up a dust rag.

"Right," Angie said. "Let's get done. I can't wait to get home to Andy."

Joan saved the bank president's office until last. She loved his big oak desk. She forgot time as she polished every surface in the room until it shone.

Angie stuck her head in the door. "We're all done, Joan. Come on, let's go home. You really should get some rest."

"You go on, dear. I'm almost done. I'll lock up, and my car is right by the back door. You have an important date to keep."

"Are you sure you're okay?" Angie asked with a worried look on her face.

"I'm just fine, now you go on. I've been closing up here for more years than I care to tell you." Joan smiled. "You go and spend every minute you can with Andy."

Angie laughed and kissed Joan on the cheek. "Okay, I'll see you tomorrow night."

Joan finished cleaning the office. Suddenly a terrible pain shot through her head. She sat down in the president's soft chair. *Just for a minute,* she told herself. She closed her eyes and dreamed about Daniel again.

Their honeymoon had been short, but very romantic. After the wedding in Salt Lake City, they rode the train back to Ogden with all of their family. Then, at Union Station, everyone rode the trolley car the few blocks to the Broom Hotel. Joan's parents had arranged a wedding dinner in the beautiful dining room of the hotel. It reminded Joan of their first real date there. After all the guests left, Joan and Daniel had gone to their room on the third floor facing the mountains, and shut the door, and the world, out.

All that was gone now, and her heart still ached when she remembered the day she lost Daniel in a farm accident twenty years earlier. She didn't really need to keep working now, but it would be hard to change her life. Her children and grandchildren filled her home and her life, but when they left, the silence was so complete it was jarring.

Joan stood up again. She needed to get home and take some aspirin. Suddenly, she realized her head didn't hurt any more. She stood up straighter, and her stiffness was gone. She reached to pick up her cleaning supplies, but the loud clang of a trolley car turned her attention to the front doors.

How strange, she thought, *there are no trolley cars here anymore*. She pulled her old worn sweater close around her shoulders. Sometimes when she was alone here at night, she heard noises. Mostly she ignored them, but she had also seen things— nothing substantial, but wispy white areas would appear, and then disappear as soon as she got close to them. As she told Angie, the "ghost" feeling was friendly and never bothered her much. But there was the sound of a trolley again. It was louder than anything she had ever heard before.

She was almost to the front door when, to her utter amazement, on the street just outside the front door, a trolley car pulled up, noisy and clanging. A man jumped down out of it and walked toward the bank. Joan panicked a little. *What if he tries to come in?* She thought. *Did Angie lock the doors?* The man indeed came to the front door. His suit was a little old-fashioned, but very nice, like he was dressed up for a wedding or something. He smiled when he saw her and waved. Joan stood frozen to the spot wondering what to do.

The man walked up to the door and opened it. Joan looked around in panic. *Maybe I've got time to call the police,* she thought. As she turned to run, she saw that her old work-worn clothes had been replaced by a beautiful old-fashioned dress, just like the dress she wore on her wedding day. She looked up and the man was standing next to her, holding his hand out to her.

He smiled and said, "Hello, Mrs. MacDonald. You are absolutely beautiful, and I've been waiting for you a very long time."

Joan gazed into those liquid brown eyes and slipped her hand into his. "Daniel, I have missed you so much," she said as tears slid down her face.

They walked slowly, arm in arm, through the lobby of the beautiful Broom hotel and up the stairs to the room facing the mountains. They went into their room and shut the door, and the world, out.

The bank president found Joan's body the next morning. She was still sitting in his chair with a peaceful smile on her face.

5. 205 ½ 25th Street

Patricia Bossano

After a forty minute delay, the plane at last takes off from San Diego.

I'm headed to Salt Lake City, and I'm feeling a bit shaky, not because I'm flying—I've made this trip countless times for business purposes—but because today, when I finish my meeting with a customer, I'm driving to Ogden, or Junction City, as it was known back in the day, when East and West were joined by the railway.

I have an appointment with Marsha, a real estate agent who's agreed to show me the property at 205 25th Street, which doesn't mean much to the average person, but to a guy like me, it is a big deal.

I was four or five years old when I first heard the name "Rosetta Duccini Davie." My grandmother told me my mom and I owed our lives to Ms. Davie.

I didn't know it then, but this was a many-layered story my grandmother would deliver, piece by piece over the years, according to her strict definition of age-appropriateness.

During my elementary school years, I knew Rosetta had been a beautiful woman, "raven-haired and red-lipped," grandmother said, and the kindest soul in the roughest of towns: Ogden in the 1940s.

My grandmother had dozens of stories about Rosetta, which she repeated whenever I asked.

Often, "Rose" was my bedtime story, and I cemented her in my mind and heart as the ideal woman for me.

I could see her, a rich lady, driving her fancy black Lincoln or walking her pet ocelot up and down 25th street—or Two-Bit Street, as it was known back then. She had been noticed and admired by everyone in Ogden, but most of all, by this elementary school boy—decades later—who nursed a secret crush for the affluent woman who helped those less fortunate, and who couldn't stand the sight of animals being mistreated.

Grandmother told me, Rose and her husband, Bill was well known for their business ventures and their passionate romance. I had mixed feelings about Bill. I tried to fit him in as a father figure in my fantasies, but I gave it up as I got older and mostly ignored that she'd had a husband.

Grandmother painted Rose as a saint, but to my ten-year-old mind, Rose was also a glamorous goddess; I saw her as a lion-tamer in the rough, circus-like world where she lived.

When I got to junior high, grandmother explained in more detail *why* my mother and I owed our lives to Rosetta.

In the 1940s, my grandmother worked at a doctor's office in Ogden to help her struggling family. She hoped to marry her boyfriend of one year whom she loved dearly. Convinced he would eventually propose, she allowed their intimacy to progress until she got pregnant. When she told him, he left her. She was only twenty-two.

Dejected and ashamed, my grandmother decided she wanted to abort the baby. She knew her family would put her on the street if she turned up pregnant—which they did. But Rosetta convinced her not to go through with it. Unable to have children of her own, Rose couldn't allow someone she knew to commit such a crime.

I remember the day my grandmother confessed this to me. "I couldn't have lived with myself if I'd gone through with the abortion," she said, and I'd never seen such remorse and sadness in someone's face. The decision she made, even if she didn't carry it out, weighed heavily on her, and I think it tormented her until the day she died.

After my mom was born, Rose made sure grandmother had extra cash, food, and clothing to help raise the baby. "If it hadn't been for Rose..." Grandmother would start, but could never complete the sentence. I think her circumstances had been so dire she couldn't stand to remember them. She would shake her head and cluck her tongue, "Rose was an angel."

Not until my early twenties did I find out who Rose had been. The knowledge was disconcerting at best, but I guess it was also satisfying because it explained why my mother never shared the same fervor for Rose my grandmother professed.

Rosetta Duccini Davie and Bill ran the classiest establishment of ill-repute on Two-Bit Street, known as The Rose Rooms—at 205 ½ 25th Street. Among other things, Rosetta required all her girls to have monthly physicals at the clinic where my grandmother worked. That was how they came to know one another.

Over the two years since I found out about Rose's profession, I have gradually come to terms with the fact that the woman I thought of as a saint had been a Madam, and only now have I worked up the courage to see the place where Rose—my ideal woman—lived and did business all those years ago.

I sometimes wonder if grandmother actually lived at 205 ½ 25th Street for a time, after her family refused to take on another mouth to feed. I think my mom wonders the same thing, but grandmother died, possibly before she thought I was old enough to know that...

(The meeting with my customer went well, though I think I was distracted. All I could think of was getting in my rental car and heading north; my head was full of Rose, and she was calling me.)

I get off the freeway on 31st Street and proceed north on Wall Avenue to the Union Station. I turn left onto 25th Street, and on the corner of Lincoln and 25th, I see the brick façade of The Rose Rooms.

The windows on the second floor gape at me.

There is a parking spot right in front of number 205, and as I pull into it, I think the ½ used in the address back in the 1940s probably referred to the second floor, but they've dropped it now.

I stare at the glass door on the left side of the building; the one leading to The Rose Rooms, which have been vacant for quite some time.

I get out of the car feeling the urge to breathe deeply—like I'm warming up for a run—completely clueless that what's coming will rip my breath away.

I'm anxious to be inside, but Marsha isn't here yet, so I press my nose to the glass and see a wooden staircase with three landings—brick walls on both sides of it. I see nothing on the first landing, but on the second, there's a door to the right.

I won't pretend the altitude is responsible for my heart beating faster. I know I'm spooked.

Rosetta and Bill lived there, I think, and I experience an odd sense of time flashing backward and forward, so fast it's actually standing still and I see in the now, everything that was, is, and will be.

A tap on my shoulder startles me.

"Sorry," says Marsha.

"Don't know why I'm so jumpy," I stammer, trying to focus on her face, but seeing only the hint of that door on the second landing. I force myself to say, "You must be Marsha."

She beams. "Yes. It's good to meet you, Fernando."

We shake hands and make small talk. I tell her I didn't have any trouble finding the place and she apologizes for the unseasonable heat; after all, it is April in Ogden, and temperatures should be cooler. I nod at this, but don't tell her I'm here precisely on the 30th anniversary of the death of a family friend.

Rosetta died on April 21, 1980, in Tampico, Mexico, where I know the weather is hot that time of year. *It's a far-fetched coincidence anyway.*

"I have a client a few doors that way," Marsha says, pointing up 25th Street. "She has some questions about a lease agreement we worked on. I thought I'd clear things up since I'm here."

I'm already nodding. "No problem."

"I'll let you in, and I'll be back in twenty minutes tops," she assures me cheerfully, digging through her purse for the keys to The Rose Rooms. When she finds them, I take them from her and open the door.

As I return the keys, Marsha says, "Look around all you want; you can't hurt anything in there. Don't trip over stuff—it's kind of messy."

"No worries, and thank you," I reply as she hurries up the street and I turn back to the staircase. I step in.

The door creaks closed behind me.

I begin to climb, trying hard not to think of myself as a regular "John" because I can't stop picturing the hundreds of men who must've come up these steps, with paper money in their pocket, looking for a little companionship. I realize I'm feeling jealous of all those men, and I mentally slap myself.

"I'm not going to the work rooms where tricks were sold," I tell myself. "I'm going to Rose's rooms."

At the height of the first landing, I detect a flowery scent—something like jasmine—which comes as a surprise inside this old building, supposedly under renovation.

By the time I reach the second landing, I can't shake the feeling I'm completely unprepared.

I go through the door, taking in every bit of the dusty surroundings. I walk toward the center of the room and accidentally step with half my foot on a two-by-four on the floor. I counter balance and before I know it, I'm flat on the ground. The back of my head throbs.

I stand up and slap the dust off my pants, glad Marsha wasn't there to see me do what she said not to. I look around and realize reason has left me completely, because I'm now in a lavish chamber decorated like a Chinese restaurant.

I see black lacquered surfaces everywhere, silver foil wallpaper with pink flowers covers one of the walls, and a mural has been painted on another.

A spotted cat, out of nowhere, slinks beneath the two windows opposite me, and leaps onto the top of a piano, side-stepping a picture frame and a vase with flowers, which have been placed atop the black instrument.

I break out in a cold sweat.

I look away from the cat, processing the fact that it might not be a cat at all. *Hell!* Inside The Rose Rooms, it would *have to be* an ocelot.

The alarming suspicion that I have walked into another dimension overwhelms me, but I can't turn back. For a moment I'm paralyzed—only my eyes swivel, taking in the sight of Rose's living space.

Near the center of the room, I see a table covered in red. There are six chairs around it. One of them has been pulled out, and I know I am invited to sit. I do so and exhale, relieved from the burden of standing, unsteady as I feel.

I sit there in the silence, hands on my knees trying to stop the shakes. My eyes are glued to the sleepily blinking ocelot, wondering if a brain scan is in order before I even return to San Diego, when the slightest creaking sound issues from the chair next to me.

The air vibrates and as I hold my breath, the air begins to take shape—it is the shape of a woman.

I've never passed out in my life but there's a first time for everything; I think this is it for me.

I recognize her. I know that long dark hair and those fiery eyes. Her creamy skin glows, and her red lips look like a wound on her smooth face. Rose.

I know I'm out of mind, at once believing and disbelieving. I can't look at her without a jumble of thoughts racing through my head: I owe Rose my life. She's a prostitute. She's the most generous soul that ever lived. She's a Madam and a lion-tamer. She's an angel, and she's sitting next to me.

Her experienced fingers knead my thigh then begin working their way up. *This is torture*, I think, and again I picture the men who paid for her touch, and I hate them. Instinctively, I press my legs together feeling this is my only defense against her insistent progress.

Part of me wonders why I should bother defending myself, but the rational—Catholic—part of me says, "Run!"

"*Mierda*," I mutter (this means "shit" in Spanish) and her laughter rings in the room, or maybe just inside my head.

"I have missed you so, Billy," she purrs, and I'm foolishly glad she's not laughing at me. Her husband, Bill, being half Mexican, must have used the expression on occasion and I had just reminded her of him.

A sense of guilt rattles me at that moment—*she called me Bill*—and right away I feel like a teen making out with his girlfriend while her parents are away. Terror grips me. What if Bill shows up and finds us? Then I think that she called *me* "Bill."

It feels like a punch to the gut. Rose might be my ideal woman, but I'm not *her* man.

A growl, something straight out of *The Exorcist*, comes from the corner of the room where the ocelot sits on top of the piano. My blood freezes in my veins.

"Don't mind her, it's just Gata. She's in heat…" Rose nuzzles my neck, and I feel her tongue there—tasting me.

Her mouth opens over my ear and she lets out a heated moan full of longing. I shudder from head to foot.

Mierda, I think. I hadn't realized my state of arousal had peaked, and now I'll need a change of pants.

I stand up abruptly, knocking the chair backwards.

I see I've hurt her feelings and I can't bear it.

Rose looks up at me, her eyes wet with tears and a pout on her lips that makes me want to carry her off to a bed and eat her up with kisses. But I won't, because if I do, it will mean I have lost myself.

"Billy," she sighs, her voice full of pain and my heart aches for her, and for me. Bitter jealousy pokes at me—*I'm not her man.*

I hesitate. Her eyes plead and I can't swallow the knot at the top of my throat. My eyes water and she becomes blurry at the edges. She looks down at her hands on her lap, and I see silver tears splash on them. "Oh, Billy," she says.

I can't take it. I scramble to my feet and back out of the room, avoiding the two-by-four this time. I stumble down the wooden stairs, splaying my arms toward the brick walls for support. I feel dizzy, possibly because I can still feel the heat of her breath, I can hear the longing in her voice, I can see the fire in her eyes. And just like when you exit the Haunted Mansion at Disneyland, I know I'm taking a stow-away ghost with me.

Out on the sidewalk, Marsha is not back yet. Through the glass door, I look back at the stairs— what would happen if I went back? What would happen if I tried to touch her? Would she say *my* name, if I asked her to?

For a few rapt moments, I think I might buy the building, live in it, and never see the light of day again. *Just turn around and do it*, I dare myself. *This is the woman for me*.

I walk a few steps back and forth; I know I'm talking myself into this. I want to. I'm sick of being alone. I want a woman with me—I want Rose. And then I stop.

I think back to my escape from The Rose Rooms—*I scrambled to my feet*, I recall and again I break out in a cold sweat. I'd been lying on the floor because of the damned two-by-four.

My brain screams this couldn't have been an unconscious experience. I can still feel her. I can still smell the jasmine—I still need a change of pants.

It's dusk and with the warm, orange radiance of the sky, the spell, the charm, the hex, the curse, whatever the hell it was, loosens its grip on me.

Refusing to look back at 205 ½, I head across the street to a bar called Brewskis. I take a seat by the window and ask the bartender for a shot of Tequila, gulping it down as soon as he brings it to me.

I stare into space until my mind quiets down. Out of the corner of my eye, I can see the brick face of The Rose Rooms. The front windows gape at me slantways—like I got away or something, and I can't help feeling I probably did.

After ditching my boxers in the men's room, and over a third shot of Tequila, I decide I will find my own raven-haired, red-lipped Rose, *but among the living.*

6. Charlie Chan and the Ben Lomond Ghost

Michael Bourn

"Lao Ye, tell me again about Mei Ling."

I had fallen asleep in the afternoon sun, sitting on the bench in front of my granddaughter's trendy new restaurant on 25th Street. She was a Chinese girl—well, to be exact, old enough to be referred to as a lady, and only part Chinese— running a sushi place, of all things, in the location of the venerable Star Noodle Parlor that had breathed its last gasp two years earlier. I loved her more than anyone. Since my dear wife died, my care and feeding fell to this lovely young woman. I especially loved to hear her call me Lao Ye— grandfather in Chinese.

"Finished with the lunch crowd?" I asked.

"All done. I have an hour before I have to get ready for the locals who come in for early dinner, and while I rest, I want to hear one of your stories."

It was our mid-afternoon ritual in nice weather—her break from a long day while the restaurant closed between three and five.

"C'mon, Lao Ye, I want to hear one of your tales of the days just after World War II, when you were Ogden's Charlie Chan, and 25th Street was a den of iniquity."

"Fancy word 'iniquity,'" I said, smiling slyly, kidding her about her good education—wasted, in my opinion, running this fancy sushi palace. But she wanted to know the restaurant business well enough to open her own place. And she was a hard worker. She would do well and perhaps provide me with much comfort in my final years, as a good Chinese granddaughter should.

"Start talking, Lao Ye," she said, widening her lovely almond-shaped eyes and grinning like the mischievous imp she'd been as a youngster.

I closed my eyes and thought back to 1946. My private investigation business had come into being a year earlier when I was an ambitious twenty-one-year-old and certain I would soon become famous. But my only customers had been Chinese, and there hadn't been many of them. Shuttering the business seemed imminent on that cold first day of November when I encountered my first white client.

"You Charlie Chan?" the large, bony round-eye asked in a quiet voice when he entered my office in a rundown building that had once been a whorehouse on Two-Bit Street.

"Fu Ho Chan's the name," I said. "But people call me Charlie. It's okay if you do the same."

"I don't care what your real name is," he said, a threatening look in his eye.

I reached into my right middle desk drawer, which I always kept open, and felt for the handle of my Smith and Wesson.

"So what can I call you?"

"If I'm paying cash, why do you need to know my name?"

"Fair enough. How can I help you?"

"I want you to find Mei Ling."

I felt a jolt at the sound of that name. Hiding my unease, I laughed. "That's easy. She's been dead four years. I can take you to her grave, if you like. Cheap. Only ten dollars."

He went pale and looked unsteady on his feet. I hurried around the desk, took him by the arm, and guided him to the only other chair in the room—the one across from my battered, metal, army-surplus desk.

"She can't be dead. I saw her last night," he said.

"Where?"

"At the Ben Lomond, in the fourth floor hallway. But she disappeared around the corner before I could catch up to her. And then she just wasn't there." His face looked like that of someone who'd witnessed an amazing magician's disappearing act.

"You're not the first," I said. "I've heard many of her former customers tell of seeing her at the hotel since returning from the war... but all of *them* were drunk."

He scowled at me. I pulled the thirty-eight from the drawer and laid it on my desk.

"I'm a Mormon. I don't drink spirits."

I laughed. "You wouldn't be the first drunk Mormon I've met, and you won't be the last. Don't worry, I won't tell your bishop. Anyway, how would a good upstanding Mormon know Mei Ling? She was, um, a lady of the evening."

He jumped from his chair, leaned over his balled-up fists he'd planted on the desk in front of me, and turned so red I thought he'd stroke right there on the spot. "Don't you ever call her that," he said, the sound of his voice as choked as though he'd just tasted one of my mom's fiery chicken concoctions.

I kept my hand on the gun but didn't pick it up.

"I apologize," I said in my most soothing tone. "Please sit down and tell me why you want to find this Chinese lady you know as Mei Ling."

He took a deep breath and sat down.

"Maybe it was another girl, and she just told you her name was Mei Ling," I said.

He shook his head. "Her name was Mei Ling. I'm sure of that."

"When did you first meet her?"

"It was 1941. Late summer. I was at Farr's Ice Cream after a long day of cutting alfalfa on my dad's farm near Hooper. She was the most gorgeous girl I'd ever seen."

"How old would you say she was?"

"Maybe fifteen."

I looked him over and took a stab at his age— he looked a lot older than me, but I supposed the war could have aged him more than his years. It had done so to many I had met since the war's end.

"And you were what—twenty?"

"Sixteen," he said with a weary grin.

That would put him at only twenty one? I was shocked but succeeded in not showing it.

"That girl couldn't have been Mei Ling. She was thirty-five when she died in 1942. Raped and beaten by four drunk soldiers home on leave. She wasn't working at the time. They picked her up at the market and took her for a ride in their convertible—out near the lake. When they'd finished with her, they left her for dead. She died in the hospital four days later, but not before being told what happened."

He went so white I might have been talking to a ghost.

"Look, it couldn't have been her," I said.

"Why not?" he said. "Chinese women often look younger than they are."

"To white people, maybe," I said. "I'm half Chinese and can tell a woman's age pretty close." Despite his tough time as a soldier, I was getting tired of the way he stereotyped my lineage.

"No offense," he said, as if reading my mind.

"Okay. Tell me about this girl at the ice cream parlor."

"She was with an elderly lady I took to be her grandmother. At first, I thought she only spoke Chinese, but when I said 'hello,' she said, 'hi.'"

He stopped there. I waited for more, but he seemed lost in the memory of that first meeting.

"So... that it?"

He shook his head. "No. No, we met twice a week from then on."

"The elderly Chinese lady always with her?" I asked.

"Just the first time. Mei Ling told me she became ill and could no longer walk that far from their house.

"And the girl was allowed out on her own? That would be pretty irregular for a fifteen-year-old Chinese girl. Her father, and particularly her mother, would never permit her to go out alone except to attend classes."

"She didn't know her father, and her mother worked in the evenings."

I could see the tears welling up in my granddaughter's eyes. She'd heard this story before, and it had made her cry then. Perhaps because she'd lost her own father at a young age—a career soldier who'd gone missing during the first Gulf War.

"If this girl that you knew as Mei Ling," I said to the man, "had truly been the daughter of the gorgeous and much sought after Mei Ling, then her father would have been one in a long string of Johns. There is a rumor that Mei Ling, in her late teens, bore a daughter. But it's never been verified."

"Was she really Mei Ling's daughter, Lao Ye?" my granddaughter asked.

"We're getting ahead of the story, sunnu?" I said.

The man asked me, "Would she have had her mother's name?"

"Probably not," I said. "Mei Ling worked as a prostitute since she was the age of the girl you met. About ten years ago, she left Electric Alley and became a courtesan. She would not have wanted her daughter to carry her name."

His face had screwed up into a question mark. "Courtesan?"

"A high-class call girl," I explained.

"Would her daughter have known?" he asked. "Mei Ling never said anything about that to me."

He looked thoughtful. "It doesn't matter. I believe you are the one to help me find her."

"Why me?"

"You'll think I'm crazy."

"Tell me," I said.

He shook his head as though trying to clear cobwebs from his mind. "I thought I heard her say, 'See Charlie Chan—he will help you,' before she disappeared."

The temperature in the room seemed to drop. I felt a wave of fear but brushed it aside.

"Okay," I said. "When did you last see *your* Mei Ling?"

"Around Christmas that year, just before I shipped out."

"And you've not seen or heard from her since then?"

"She wrote a few times. Then her letters stopped."

"When was this?" I asked.

"Late 1942. I was in the Pacific."

"POW?"

"Yeah."

"Why'd you wait so long to look for her? You must have been freed a year or more ago."

He looked down. "Hospital. Took me all this time to regain my strength and enough weight not to look like a scarecrow."

"Okay," I said. "I'll look for her. My rate's fifty dollars a day."

He looked at me as though I'd said a thousand. Fifty was the rate for white clients, twenty for Chinese.

"I'll require a week in advance," I said. I felt sorry for him, but I also needed the money—my wife was expecting our first child.

He stood and peeled five fifties from a roll that looked like it held several thousand dollars.

"Better be careful carrying that around," I said.

"My back pay," he said, holding up the wad of bills.

When he left the office, I telephoned my wife. She was at first delighted with the money, but when I told her about the case, she became upset.

"Maybe you should give it back," she told me.

"Can't. We need it. You can't keep working much longer. Besides, I feel sorry for him. He's had a rough time of it. Maybe something can be arranged…"

The other end of the line was silent for a few moments, then my wife said, "Maybe you should consult her mother's ghost." She hung up on me.

I decided to sleep at my uncle's place behind the Utah Noodle Shop on Washington the next few days. Going home was out of the question until my wife cooled off. One of the stereotypes of Chinese women that run true to form is that of a fiery temper. And my wife was above and beyond in that regard.

I went to the Ben Lomond late that night. I wanted to check out the rumors of Mei Ling's ghost. The security guard was a friend. He took me to the fourth floor around midnight and left me alone. I walked up and down the hall for more than two hours and never saw a ghost, but I had the eerie feeling of being watched the entire time. More than once I thought I heard soft, high-pitched laughter like small tinkling bells in a light breeze.

My client didn't turn up again until two weeks later.

"Where've you been?" I asked.

"Sick. Then just walking the streets, looking at faces."

"Find her?" I asked, my heart rate rising.

"No sign. No one knows of a Mei Ling. Except for the one you mentioned."

I let out the breath I'd been holding. "I haven't found anything either. You want me to keep looking?"

He peeled off another five fifties and handed them to me. "I'm running out of time," he said.

"You going somewhere?"

"You could say that. The docs tell me."

"How long?" I asked, feeling like a heel for taking his money.

"Couple months. At best. My lungs are shot."

"And you want to see this girl again before you check out. That it?"

"Yeah. The thought of coming home, meeting her again, maybe getting married... that's what kept me going."

"Even though you didn't hear from her all that time?"

"She thought I was dead. I didn't know it while I was a POW, but everyone in my platoon was declared killed in action not long after we were captured. I learned about it in the hospital, when I was recovering."

I hesitated, my pulse rising. "What if she's already married?"

"That's probably best. I'm not going to be around. I just want to see her. Tell her what she meant to me all that time in the camps."

My granddaughter laid her hand gently on my arm. I smiled at her; she looked so like her grandmother.

"What did you do next?" she asked.

"That evening, I talked to your grandmother about the man looking for Mei Ling. His terrible situation made her cry, and she agreed to help. But I had no way to contact him. He hadn't left me an address or telephone number, and I assumed he didn't want someone from the Chinese community searching for him around Hooper. I still didn't know his name. Fortunately, he returned to the office three days later."

The man looked worse than before. He whispered, "Have you found her?"

"I think I can arrange a meeting," I told him, realizing his time was growing short.

"When? Where?"

"Tonight at the Utah Noodle Parlor on Washington Boulevard—ten o'clock, just after closing. Can you be there?"

He nodded, and I left to make the arrangements.

That night, I waited on the street as my uncle turned the open sign to closed and switched off most of the lights. It was a quarter after ten, and the man hadn't shown. Fifteen minutes later, I was about to leave when a cab stopped at the curb.

The passenger door opened, and a wheezing voice said, "Give me a hand."

I helped my client from the car. My uncle opened the door and seated us at a table in the center of the restaurant against the south wall. He brought us a pot of green tea and three cups. I was pouring for the two of us when I noticed my client looking over my shoulder, an expression on his face as if he'd seen an angel. A pregnant Chinese woman approached from the shadows. I took my tea and went to another table.

When he spoke her name, it was as though he whispered a prayer, "Mei Ling."

He stood as she came to the table and held out his hands for hers. I could see the tears roll down his face when her hands met his. They sat and began to whisper.

Their meeting lasted for no longer than ten minutes, and I saw how he slumped when she rose from the table and walked toward the back of the restaurant.

I went to the table. "Ready?" I asked.

He nodded, and I helped him up.

We shuffled to the door. I turned the lock and opened it. The cab waited at the curb.

"Was it worth it?" I asked.

He looked at me, and I could see the answer in his eyes. Seldom had I seen anyone look so much at peace.

"Here, take this," he said.

I looked down and saw the big stack of bills. I pushed his hand away. "I can't."

"You told me your wife was pregnant. Go ahead, take it. You'll need it. I offered it to Mei Ling, but she refused."

"You're sure you want to do this?" I looked back toward the noodle shop to see if anyone was watching. The restaurant was dark.

"Please," he pleaded. "I'm not going to need it, and my family is well enough off that it would mean nothing to them."

I opened my hand and felt the money fall onto my palm. I closed my fingers around the wad and opened the car door for him. That was the last time I saw him.

Shadows grew long on Historic 25th Street where I sat with my lovely granddaughter. She looked at me with those soulful eyes of hers.

"The ghost—did you ever see her?" she asked.

"Not at that time or for many, many years after. But now I see both her and her daughter often. We even talk, now and then."

My granddaughter tilted her head and looked at me as she would at an odd curiosity.

I waved a hand and laughed. "Crazy Lao Ye, huh?"

She smiled and gave me a one-armed hug. Then she asked, "Did you ever learn your client's name?"

"Much later."

"How?"

She had asked this question before, and I had not answered it. Perhaps it was time she knew.

"Your grandmother told me."

7. A Good Yarn

Drienie Hattingh

I t was the fourth Thursday of the month—knitting night at The Needle Point Joint on Historic 25th Street in Ogden, Utah.

Annette had finished working at 5 p.m. at the Ogden Union Station where she was an event planner. Now she sat among her fellow knitters, happily knitting away in one of her favorite stores on this street.

She hardly heard the conversation while focused on the difficult pattern—a cable sweater for her husband—knitting the cuff of the second sleeve. It had been a long process. She had started knitting it in March and wanted it be done before Christmas, which was a month away.

Annette's grandmother, who taught her to knit, had told her, 'If you knit, you will never be bored.' She and her friends, Janet, Pat, and Rosemary knitted for several charities including the Knit for Kids Program and the Pregnancy Care Center as well as knitting hats for Ogden's homeless. In-between they knitted items for family and friends.

"What will your next project be, Annette?" Pat asked with a smile as she turned over a lovely blue baby blanket to begin the next row. It was almost done, and it covered Pat's whole lap.

"I'm not sure," Annette said. "I'm almost finished with the projects I had planned for this year—the shawls and John's sweater." She had also knitted five sweaters for the Knit for Kids Program and some booties for the Pregnancy Care Center.

"I guess it is November," she said, "so I might as well start knitting the hats."

Having said that, Annette got up, walked to the back of the store, and pulled two balls of red yarn from the shelves. They were a blend of nylon and acrylic. She walked to the counter in the front of the store and paid for them before returning to the table.

"I already knitted five hats," Janet said, as she sewed up the seam of another one. "This makes six, and I used up all the leftover yarn from the little sweaters."

"You sure did knit up a storm these last months," Rosemary piped up, as she continued knitting the sweater for the Knit for Kids Program, "I cannot believe you knitted forty of those shawls, Annette! I do love the one you knitted for me."

"You should have seen Rosemary and me at church last Sunday!" Darla said with a huge smile. "We wore our shawls and lots of people complimented us on them."

Darla wasn't a knitter and usually brought office work with her on knitting nights. She only attended because she was Rosemary's ride. Rosemary was blind. This fact did not prevent her from winning first prize at the State Fair for one of her sweaters.

Annette smiled. She enjoyed knitting the shawls. It was on her so-called "Bucket List" to knit a sweater for all the special women in her life. After knitting five or six shawls, she didn't have to look at the pattern anymore; she knew it by heart and could even watch Lifetime Movies while knitting them. After finishing the shawl project and now putting the finishing touches to John's sweater, she felt a little bit at a loss. She could not imagine *not* knitting, but frankly she wasn't in the mood to knit hats and Christmas was still a long way off.

An idea took shape as she folded John's finished sweater. She wanted to knit something special for her daughter Karen, something extraordinary. A couple of weeks before she looked through the new winter pattern books and one book caught her attention... *The Unofficial Harry Potter Knits.* The book was filled with patterns based on clothing the characters in the Harry Potter movies wore. Sweaters, shawls, hats, socks... but what really made Annette sit up straight was the pattern for the so-called 'invisible hooded cloak.' She knew Karen would love that. She grew up reading the Harry Potter books and loved the subsequent movies. The only problem was the pattern... it was lace... Annette had never knitted lace before. Whenever she saw a lace pattern, she thought it was crochet. Only recently had she realized lace could be knitted.

The following day, during her lunch break, Annette walked to The Needle Point Joint. She sat at the huge table in the back of the store paging through the Harry Potter magazine until she came to the 'invisible cloak' pattern. *It is so beautiful*, she thought. The young woman who modeled the cloak, peeked from under the hood, and the cloak reached right down to her ankles. One button, at the front, held the cloak in place. It looked oh-so-delicate. She looked at the pattern but couldn't make heads or tails of it. These weren't ordinary instructions. The chart looked like something between tick-tack-toe and a word puzzle. Would she be able to knit something so intricate?

She stood up and walked over to Deanna, one of the attendants. "Can you explain this to me?" she asked, pointing at the chart.

"Oh, it's a chart—the instructions for the shawl. It's actually easy, once you understand it."

Deanna explained to Annette how to read the pattern, but try as she might, Annette couldn't wrap her mind around it. Although, she just could not let it go either. She kept on seeing her daughter's face in her mind's eye as she opened her gift under the Christmas tree and laid eyes on the cloak. She would be in heaven and wouldn't believe that her mother could have knitted it. Annette made up her mind. *I will knit the cloak, however difficult it might be.* She paid for the magazine and while deep in thought, she walked back up 25th Street to the Union Station.

That afternoon wasn't busy so she sat at her desk and again opened the magazine at the pattern, trying to figure it out, but she just couldn't. After she locked her office door at the end of the day, she decided to quickly drop by the knitting shop. Even if she still didn't understand the pattern, she wanted to buy the yarn.

As she walked across the cobble stones in front of historic Union Station, she looked at her watch— Needle Point closes in five minutes! She ran up the street to the yarn shop. She just had to have the yarn today. But she came to stand in front of a locked door.

"Oh, shoot!" she mumbled as she walked away.

Then she heard a click behind her and turned back.

A gray-haired little lady peeked at her through a small opening in the door.

"May I help you, my dear?" she asked in a Scottish accent.

"I wanted yarn for a new project, but I guess I'll have to come back tomorrow." Annette said miserably.

"We are closed," said the lady, and then winked at Annette. "But I know how you feel. I am a knitter too and I know how it is when you are anxious to start on a new pattern. I'm sure you won't be able to sleep tonight, if you are like me." She smiled kindly as she opened the door wide.

"Oh... thank you so much," Annette said as she walked into the dimly-lit store. She quickly opened the magazine to the cloak pattern and showed it to the woman.

"Mmmm... that sure is lovely," she smiled warmly at Annette with twinkling eyes. "I have the perfect yarn for the pattern," she said, beckoning Annette to follow. They walked past shelves filled with yarn, grouped by color and name brand.

Annette heard a scraping sound and frowned. Then she noticed one of the lady's legs was enclosed in a steel harness, which made walking difficult. Her steel-encased boot dragged across the floor, making scraping sounds as she went. But it didn't bother Annette. She felt strangely content. *She's wearing the same soft lilac fragrance Grandmother used*, she thought happily.

"Here we are!" the lady said as she reached for a beautiful burgundy-colored thick twist of yarn. "Silk and merino," she whispered to Annette, as if it was a secret. "You'll need 5 skeins for this pattern."

Annette drew her breath in. This was Karen's favorite shade of red! But Annette sighed... knowing this was the section where the expensive yarn was kept—anything from $20 to $40 for one skein—something she just could not afford.

The little old lady put the twist of yarn in her hands. It was lovely and soft, and the color was so enticing. The yarn felt warm and silky in her hands. Then she saw the price: $37!

"Gosh," she said, while admiring it. "It's exquisite, but I'll have to look at cheaper yarn; this is too expensive.

"You should always use the best possible yarn, especially when you knit such a time-consuming, intricate pattern! You are going to spoil it all with an inferior yarn!"

Annette was surprised when she detected underlying anger in the old woman's voice. Nevertheless, she went to the section with the cheaper yarn and looked at every color. Behind her, she heard the scraping sound as the old woman walked to the counter.

The yarn in her hands felt coarse in comparison to the silk and merino yarn. But she had to be content with the inferior yarn; John would kill her if she spent that much money. He just didn't get it and told her more than once, "You can go and buy a knitted garment for less than you spend on the yarn! Why go through all that trouble knitting it, wasting time and money?"

Annette walked to the counter and set down the yarn. The color was redder than she wanted and she sighed again, knowing the expensive yarn would have been perfect. The old lady looked at the yarn on the counter, shaking her head in a disapproving manner. She placed it in a sack and rang it up. It came to less than half the price of the other yarn. Some of the excitement in the project had gone. As Annette walked out of the store, she thanked the lady, but in her mind, she thought, *you spoiled it all, I'll keep thinking of the good yarn as I'm knitting.*

It was surprisingly dark outside. Annette hadn't realized she had spent so much time in the store. She thought she'd wave goodbye to the lady, but was surprised to see the dark interior.

That night Annette, now much less enthusiastic about her new project, decided not to struggle with the pattern quite yet and instead made one of John's favorite meals—fish and chips.

She would ask Pat at the next knitting night to help her with the pattern. Pat was a much better knitter and she could explain a difficult pattern in much simpler terms than most.

***

It was a snowy Thursday night in Ogden when the next knitting evening at The Needle Point Joint rolled around.

As soon as everyone settled down, knitting projects in their hands, Annette reached for the sack holding the yarn and the knitting magazine. "Can you please help me, Pat?" she said as she spread the magazine in front of her. "Have you ever seen anything like this?"

"Oh, yes," Pat said pulling her face into an I-don't-have-a-clue expression.

"You can't help me?" Annette asked.

"No... I'm sorry." Pat said, "I tried it before but it's so, so difficult. I think you should ask Verna or Deanna for help, or ask Randy—you know what a good knitter he is! But, please, show us the yarn!"

Annette sighed as she reached for the yarn. "It's nothing special..." She started to say and then froze. Before she even saw the yarn, she knew it wasn't the cheap yarn. Her fingers closed around the twisted silk and merino yarn—soft and warm. She slowly pulled it out of the bag.

"Oh my goodness," Janet said. "That's lovely! I just want to curl up with it! It must have cost a lot."

Pat held it close, "I just want to hug it!"

Rosemary heard all the excitement and held out her hands, "Let me feel it, let me feel it!"

The knitters always went crazy over a good yarn. And Annette looked on in mystified horror as they passed the expensive yarn from one pair of hands to the other. Her friends fingered and caressed it while they ooh'd and aah'd. And Rosemary lifted it to her face and held it against her cheek. "It's lovely," she said with wonder in her unseeing eyes.

"Annette stammered. "This... isn't the yarn I bought... I... I don't know how it got into the bag. The old lady put the cheaper yarn in, not this one."

"What old lady?" Darla, Janet, and Pat asked at the same time.

Annette told them of her experience that night, how she had gotten there after closing and how the old woman had opened the door. She explained how the woman had taken her straight to the expensive yarns and that she, Annette, had said she couldn't afford it, and finally, that the lady seemed offended when she chose the cheap yarn.

"I saw the lady put the cheap yarn into the sack. I really did!" She said again, totally confused.

"Well, I never!" said Pat. "How can that be?"

"You must be mistaken," Darla said. "Perhaps you had both the yarns on the counter, and the lady put the wrong yarn in the sack?"

"No…" Annette said. "I never brought the expensive yarn to the counter. I put it right back on the shelf before I walked all the way down to the other end of the store…"

"The receipt," Janet said. "Look at the receipt!"

Annette frantically looked inside the sack and was relieved to find it. She glanced at it and her eyes grew round in surprise. "It's the receipt for the cheap yarn. I told you I didn't buy this yarn," she ended in a whisper. "Gosh, I'll have to show this to Verna or Deanna. I hope they won't think I stole it!"

Rosemary reached for Annette's hand. "Don't worry. They know you. They'll never think that of you! I'm sure there's a rational explantation."

"Ooh... I know... " Darla said. "It must be one of those infamous ghosts on 25th Street; The Needle Point Joint is haunted, you know!"

"What are you talking about?" Annette asked.

"Oh, perhaps you weren't here when Deanna and Verna told us!" With big dramatic eyes, Darla whispered, "They say sometimes, when they come into the store, balls of yarn are scattered on the floor. And sometimes, when Verna opens the store in the morning, she hears scraping sounds, as if someone is dragging a steel object over a cement floor. She says she's the only person in the building when this happens." She continued, "And Randy once told me that one day, they were all in the front of the store, when they heard the back door open and heard footsteps. The back door was locked and they never did see the person who entered."

Everyone looked at Darla, not believing her.

Annette's throat had gone dry. She shook her head, and thought, *don't be silly... you don't believe in that stuff!*

"Ask Verna and Deanna!" Darla said. "I also heard that a lady, who used to work here and who died many years ago, hated synthetic yarns, and the yarn they sometimes find on the floor of the shop, is mostly made of nylon! Perhaps it's her ghost who's bumping the cheap yarns from the shelves, and perhaps she switched the yarn in your bag."

"What if it's so? Perhaps it was this ghost who you talked to, Annette." Janet giggled.

Annette only smiled a little at her friends' comments. She didn't think it was funny. She was glad she hadn't told them about the scraping sound the lady made with her steel-encased boot. Regardless, she wanted to get to the bottom of this. She'll ask Verna about the mysterious old woman.

Rosemary was still holding the beautiful yarn and was now pressing it to her nose and inhaling deeply. "It smells like lavender!" She held the yarn up to where she felt Annette's presence.

Here you are my dear."

Annette hesitantly took the yarn from her friend. She found it difficult to breath. The yarn *did* smell like lavender.

Pat looked at her watch. "I must go! You'll have to tell us all about the outcome next time, Annette."

"Yes, me, too. See you all next time," Janet said as she pushed her knitting back into her bag. Everyone hugged, and Pat held the door open as Darla guided Rosemary outside.

Annette walked to the counter.

"Hi, Annette, "Verna said, "Do you need yarn for that lovely lace shawl?"

Annette explained all that had happened with the old lady and the expensive yarn she didn't buy.

"That's strange; we don't have anyone like that working here."

"But she was here! Look, here's the yarn. I saw her put the cheap yarn in the sack. Honestly, I don't know where the expensive yarn came from."

Verna inspected the label then shook her head.

"We don't carry that particular brand in the store. Ooh... it is lovely, though, isn't it?" she said as she fingered the yarn.

"But, look," Annette said, showing Verna the receipt.

"Yes, I can see it's a receipt from the store, but look at the date. You bought two balls of red yarn at the last meeting, remember? You said you were going to knit hats for the homeless."

"But ... I ... saw her ..." Annette stammered.

"Why fret about where the yarn came from?" Verna said with a smile. "Just think of it as a beautiful gift and enjoy it and start knitting the amazing cloak for your daughter!"

Annette felt dizzy.

"You look pale," Verna said. "Sit down, I'll bring you some water, and I'll take these lovely skeins of yarn and spin it into a workable ball on the swift in the back."

Annette sat down at the table. The knitting magazine was still open at the lace cloak pattern. As if in a dream, she looked at the funny chart with the little squares and crosses and circles and just like that—she understood it all.

Verna came back with the water and nicely wound ball of soft, silky burgundy yarn.

"Here you go. All ready to knit. Do you want me to explain again how this chart works?"

"No, thanks, Verna... I understand it all now," Annette said with a radiant smile. She took the knitting needles from her knitting bag. She made a loop on the left needle with the yarn and cast on the correct number of stitches, as the pattern instructed. Then she started to knit.

"Stay as long as you want, Annette," Verna said, "Deanna, Randy and I are taking inventory downstairs, and we'll be here for at least another couple hours. And oh, I have some new yarn in—a mixture of nylon and acrylic in lovely bright colors. I thought it would be perfect for knitting the little sweaters and the hats and—"

"Verna, I will never...!" Annette said in a shrill voice... then she stopped. She realized she was very angry and could not think why. But she swallowed some water, and then said in a much nicer voice,

"Sorry, Verna, but I've decided to never knit with an inferior yarn again."

Verna smiled mischievously. "It looks as if you believe all the spooky little lady told you."

But Annette did not hear her anymore. She was absorbed in the lace pattern. She knitted continuously, effortlessly, barely looking at the pattern, as snow sifted down outside the window of The Needle Point Joint.

With a knowing smile, she inhaled softly. The lilac scent relaxed as well as comforted her while her fingers worked the needles.

***

Christmas Eve was a lovely snowy day in Ogden. Annette and John were happy to have their daughter home from college for Christmas break.

Karen helped Annette to clear the table after reading the Christmas story and enjoying a wonderful meal. Then she set the table with her mother's best porcelain tea things.

Annette put the special desserts in the middle, next to the candles. According to tradition, they would have tea and dessert after opening presents.

They gathered around the sparkling tree.

Annette was thrilled with the beautiful sapphire ring John had given her, her birthstone. She held it up against the Christmas tree lights and it sparkled brilliantly. John looked pleased that she was so happy.

Then she opened Karen's gift, a lovely knitting basket to keep all her projects in, filled with fragrant bath soaps and salts.

John loved the sweater she had knitted for him. He immediately pulled it over his head and hugged and kissed her. "I cannot believe you actually knitted this, especially for me... all the time you must have spent knitting it!"

His gratitude warmed her heart.

Karen opened an envelope John gave her.

"Merry Christmas!" he said with a smile.

It was a check, as usual. Karen yelped at the amount and hugged her father fiercely.

Finally, Annette handed Karen her gift.

Karen was speechless as she held the soft silky cloak to her face, inhaling deeply.

"It smells like lilacs! It is so lacy, so soft, so, so beautiful—I've never seen anything like it!"

Karen listened in awe to her mother as she explained that it was the 'invisible cloak' from Harry Potter. Annette did not bother them with the finer details, on how she acquired the yarn and the mysterious woman.

Karen put the cloak on and twirled around and around. "Mom, I'll treasure it forever."

Annette's eyes filled with tears when John hugged her again, and said. "I understand now. You spent countless hours knitting these gifts for us, with love in every stitch. That is the real gift."

Annette's eyes shifted from her happy little family and came to rest on the falling snow out their window. "Thank you, dearest lady," she whispered, "whoever you are, for helping me with the pattern... and teaching me all about a good yarn."

8. Goodbye Mary Belle

Fred Seppi

C oming to this address is quickly becoming a habit that has to stop. For the third time this week, I find my car parked in front of 246 25th Street in Ogden to have Tony make one of his delicious arrabiata (spicy) pizzas, anchovies and all, to go. Today, the interior of the bar is too noisy with all the stampede music on full blast, so I prefer to wait the twenty minutes in the car listening to my choice of noise.

On other days of the week, I do wait inside at a table that allows my memory of this tavern interior to roam over the many years in youth spent here polishing the brown oak twenty-foot bar to a glistening sheen, and making sure the tile floor showed no markings of the numerous regurgitations that may have embedded themselves in the tile grout by people who downed more beer than they were capable of handling. Weekly washing of the two big front windows, the back door window, and all the mirrors was also on the agenda.

Today, this tavern is called Brewskis. But in my youth, it was the National Tavern, proudly owned and managed for forty years by my father, who was known to everyone as Freddie. For some reason, I also acquired that name from all my friends and working associates. It was undoubtedly an impression both our puerile personalities fostered.

The first day I became the chief weekly janitor for this tavern; my father showed me around and listed the duties he expected. Of course, the most important job included making sure the dark-brown varnish on the bar was spotless and reflected every ray of the morning sun peering through the glass door and south windows. The windshield, as the inventor Oscar Wilde had said, "should be able to avoid cold blasts of wind entering through the opened front door in the winter but also should discourage in the summer the curious gazing through the front window by lonely wives who might seek to prove an unfeeling husband lurking in the pub to talk politics or other gossip with his associates rather than being home to read bedtime stories to his children."

In addition to the work assignments, there were a few precautions my father advocated. One was regarding the door on the east wall adjacent to the front window. That door is always locked and should remain so. Only once did I go through that door. My father had to deliver some mail to the grocer down the street, and curiosity overtook my good judgment. I opened the door to find that turning in one direction led to a large sign, with the name of the famous rodeo town, Cheyenne, printed in giant red letters, misspelled as SHY ANNE.

In the opposite direction were the stairs leading to the top two floors of the building. These floors were managed by a lady I came to know endearingly as Mary Belle. This was not her real name. I knew because she was the daughter of my mother's friend, who had been in mother's elementary school district in Trentino, Italy, before both teenage girls came to America with their families many years before.

Straight ahead was a third stairway leading down to the basement where the stock rooms for each establishment on the street were located. A rough elevator was situated underneath the outer sidewalk. The elevator shaft had a steel cover door that would rise up when the elevator was to be loaded to provide a convenient routing for heavy merchandise to be lowered to the stock rooms of each establishment on both 25th Street and Washington Boulevard. For my dad's bar, the heavy beer kegs were located in this basement area and the liquid piped to the faucets lining the inside of the bar upstairs.

I noticed the elevator was enclosed with ornamental cement work that seemed inappropriate for such dreary stockroom surroundings. Since someone had once mentioned the tunnel to me that ran under 25th Street, from the Hotel Ben Lomond to the Union Station, I quickly backtracked through the door I had opened, and made no mention of my findings to my father.

While out in the car, awaiting the time when the pizza would be ready to be picked up, I fell asleep at the wheel and was rudely awakened by a pounding on the car front window by a lady in a beautiful formal blue gown. "You look very familiar to me, sonny. You don't happen to be Freddie's son, do you? You know we used to call your father

Freddie because he never seemed to age."

"Yes, I suppose I am. And who are you?"

"Do you remember the winter I was always afraid you were working too hard delivering drugs on your bicycle in the cold and I made you sit down and rest with a cup of hot chocolate and some panetti before continuing your deliveries?"

"Yes, I do remember. Each of my deliveries to your apartment meant a half hour of rest time before the next stop. There was always a generous tip for the delivery from you or the other girls in the building. And remember I told you how those teenagers who parked at the curb would laugh when I would go down to the sidewalk, unlock my bike, and try to peddle away before they would ask me why I took so long to deliver the medicine and how much it cost me? Once the bike was unlocked, I would yell back to them I was just drinking cocoa and even got a quarter tip. But I could hear their laughter all the way along the three blocks up to Washington Boulevard. How I hated those older teenagers who were going to Weber College and thought they were so sophisticated.

"And the last I saw you, you gave me a twenty dollar bill to buy books when I told you I had quit my job at Owl Drug to go to Weber College next quarter. You made me take it and it has never been repaid."

"No, there is no need for money anymore. I am just so happy to have been able to see you once again, Freddie."

"My mother and I noticed your mother's obituary in the Standard Examiner five years ago and both attended the funeral. Your father had died about one year earlier. They were so devoted to each other it must have been difficult for your mother to have continued without him."

Mary Belle agreed.

"Where are you living now, Mary Belle?"

"Here in my old rooms on the third floor, where you used to come with your deliveries and drink the hot chocolate."

"On the third floor? I heard there was a fire on that floor, so people are only allowed to live on the second floor."

"Oh, I manage by myself very well on the third. But please, don't you try to go past the barricades and signs saying "Keep out! Danger!" The footing is really not safe for most human traffic."

"Since I have not seen you after my last day of work at the Owl Drug, you must want to know how I got back at those teenagers razzing me on the curb down here in front of your door.

"When they taunted me about the time and the cost of that last visit, I simply told them I was with you about an hour, and you gave me a twenty dollar bill for all the services I had rendered over the years. With the bike already unlocked and ready to go, I sped away without hearing any laughter."

But before leaving Mary Belle for the last time, I told her how during my youth; I had kept up with her exploits recorded in the local newspaper. We both remembered our first meeting when she came in her beautiful car to our house on Washington Boulevard to explain something to my mother that could have damaged my parents' marriage until Mother heard Mary Belle's explanation. From then on, I followed her ventures however the newspaper decided to portray them.

"Tell me how to get up to your apartment, and I will stop to see you tomorrow. We have so much to talk about. So many years have gone by."

"Look at the time. You better go in to get your pizza. Tony gets mad if people don't pick up pizza right when it's ready to go. We will see each other soon."

When I returned to the car with the pizza, Mary Belle was gone. For some reason, I thought it appropriate to drive to the grave site of her mother and father to wish them well. The entire family had one plot with individual head stones.

One stone read, Mom P. 1967, another, Dad P. 1965, and another, Son P. 1941. But the fourth marker was the heart stopper: Mary Belle P. 1975.

On February 13, 1923, the 36-year-old Union Station, went up in flames.

February 14, 1923. Ogden Standard Examiner
"....the squatty, poorly lighted, ill-vented, unattractive old depot will now be replaced."

9. The Legend of the
Union Station Fire

Christy Monson

An undisclosed ghostly source has just uncovered the real cause of the 1923 Union Station Fire.

Tuesday, February 13, 1923

A light bulb shattered and sent glass shards plummeting toward the floor. Waiting passengers in the Union Station lobby glanced upward and ducked. Another light bulb blew apart. The lights flickered. Travelers screamed, brushing glass shards from their hair and faces. They ran out the doors—

some toward the train yard tunnel and others toward the shiny Model T's letting passengers off in front of the station.

The General glanced up at the ceiling.

"Leave those lights alone, Half-pint" he said. A young boy dressed in holey overalls floated behind a ceiling beam. "And stop pretending to smack the ball out of the park with your stick. You got dusty glass on my coat, and you're chasing all the pretty girls away."

"Just creating atmosphere, General," said Half-pint, laughing.

General flicked specks of dust and glass from his shoulders where he sat in his overstuffed rocker near the middle of the lobby. "This is such an ill-vented, unattractive place. Wish it would burn down," he said as he hunkered into the velvety soft chair. He wished everyone would leave him to his pastime of enjoying the ladies. Being a retired ghost was the best death of all.

The screaming and commotion over, a lady with a flare skirt sauntered his way. Her hat had a gaudy arrangement of pheasant feathers on it. General lifted her skirt. "Almost as nice as Madame." He rubbed his whiskered chin. "Now she gives the 25th Street ghosts real class."

"Thanks for the compliment," said a rich, throaty voice, floating in the side window.

"Madame." General turned in his chair. "To what do we owe this pleasure?"

Madame's bouffant red hair cascaded over her slinky red dress. "Let's stir up some trouble. Things are too quiet here on Two-Bit Street."

The General pulled her onto his lap. "But I'm retired, and I'm not moving from this chair—ever."

"Have it your way." Madam tickled her finger through the General's hair. "You're missin' out. I'm going to give the people around here a good scare."

"Scare?" Half-pint floated down to join them. "I'm always looking for fun."

"Follow my lead, boy," said Madame. "Let's find a way to get the General to join us in spookin' up this street. It's way too quiet."

"Never." General pulled Madame to him in a kiss. "You can come see me anytime. But I'm not leaving here. I'm planted."

"We'll see about that." Madame pulled away and danced around his chair.

The light gray film of a Salvation Army sergeant descended from the ceiling with an open Bible in his hands. "General, I can tell you have unclean thoughts entering your mind."

General shifted in his chair. "Churchy, get lost. You're ruining my fun."

Madame turned to Churchy. "We don't need you tellin' us to stay out of trouble."

"Just trying to instill a sense of morality in you." Churchy snapped his Bible shut. "Choir's practicing in a few minutes. Join us and cleanse your life."

"I do *not* need a lecture on virtue," said General. "I'm a big boy now, and I can sit here and enjoy the scenery—and... " he snatched the corner of Madame's dress and drew her to him, "those who are kind enough to come my way."

Madame brushed the General away and danced around Churchy, tousling his hair. "I could use a handsome guy like you in my corner. Why don't you join Half-pint and me?"

"Remember, clean hands and a pure heart." Churchy backed away, floating up the stairs and through the roof. "Too hot for me here. I'm going to sing with the angels."

General shook his head and muttered to himself. "Who needs enemies when I have friends like Churchy and Half-pint to disturb me?" He settled in to wait for another lady to walk by.

The lights flickered again.

Madame wafted toward the second floor. "Follow me, Half-pint. Let's disturb the General."

"What about the passengers in the station?" Half-pint followed Madame.

"We'll get 'em all." Madame laughed. "That's the fun of it."

"General makes me mad," said Half-pint. "He's always on my case."

"You're cute," said Madame. "How did you come among us riffraff?"

"Burned up in a house fire," said Half-pint. "It's a horrible way to go."

"Poor baby." Madame sighed. "We all have a tale to tell."

"It doesn't matter how you bit the dust," said Churchy, peering through the ceiling. "Just get up and go on."

"Eavesdropping?" Madame turned to look up.

Half-pint sighed. "Churchy gives me no sympathy." He floated toward the station manager's office on the second floor. "I have an idea."

"I'm right behind you," said Madame.

"Now don't go making trouble," said Churchy.

"Join us or get lost," said Madame.

"I'll tag along to keep you out of trouble."

"Make up your mind," said Half-pint, wafting into the first office. "I'm going to use the inkwells for baseball practice."

"What's that rapscallion doing now?" called General from the lobby.

"Leave me alone." Half-pint clunked the lid off an inkwell.

"Wait." Madame put her hand up to stop him. "I have a better idea." She picked up the dark blue inkwell and got several more from the closet. "Let's take them to the lobby and use them for ball practice. I'll pitch."

"Great," said Half-pint.

"Ahhh," Churchy snapped his Bible open and shut again. "Inky-blue patrons await us."

The three wafted toward the lobby with Madame carrying the bottles. Half-pint grabbed his stick from the ceiling beam.

General sat in his chair below the clock tower blowing smoke from a man's cigar toward a baby. The infant coughed and sneezed.

Churchy hovered above. "Stop that! You're spewing filthy smoke into a child's face."

"Thanks for pointing that out to me," said General.

Churchy stamped his foot in midair. "As you sow, so shall you reap."

"Get lost," said General.

Churchy snapped his Bible shut and opened it again.

Madame steadied herself at one end of the lobby above the passengers' heads and signaled Half-pint to the other side of the room.

Madame wound up and whipped the inkwell toward Half-pint. He hit it, spattering glass and blue ink across the room. Madame pitched another and another. *Smack, smack.*

People scattered, screaming again.

"It's blue rain," said a little boy.

His mother grabbed him and rushed outside. She tried to brush the drops off her skirt and smeared inky streaks all over her.

General looked at his jacket and then at Madame. "That's not funny. You've ruined my good coat."

Madame laughed. "Come to my place, and I'll clean you up." She waggled her hips.

"I told you I'm not leaving this chair," said General. "I'm retired."

Half-pint floated toward him. "Home run hits, huh, General?"

General looked up at him. "I wish you didn't have such a good arm."

"What about me? I'm the one with the good arms." Madame waved them toward General.

"I don't care what you do," said General. "I'm not moving."

"We'll see about that." Madame linked her arm through Half-pint's and wafted toward the north wing of the building.

"What are you up to now?" asked Churchy.

Madame whisked Half-pint through the wall into a hotel room. Churchy followed.

A glowing kerosene lamp sat on the desk. Light shone under the bathroom door, and they could hear the bathwater running in the tub.

"Why is there an oil lamp in here?" asked Half-pint. "There's electricity in these rooms."

"Ah," said Churchy. "It's hard for a leopard to change its spots."

"What does that mean?" asked Half-pint.

"Some folks have a hard time with new inventions," said Madame.

"Well," said Half-pint, "I want to check out this kerosene lamp, how do they work?" He lifted the glass and tipped the lamp. Oil dripped onto the desk.

"Careful, you could start a fire." Churchy pulled Half-pint away from the lamp, causing a draft that knocked the glass onto the floor where it shattered. "More broken glass."

"Now you've done it," said Half-pint, sliding through the wall into the hall. "If a fire starts, it'll be your fault."

"Great idea," said Madame. "That's how we'll get General out of his chair and spookin' up Two-Bit Street.

"Not fire," said Half-pint, shivering. "I hate fire."

"Fire can't hurt you now," said Madame. "You're already dead."

"Fires still send quivers through me."

Madame tipped the lamp so the flame ignited the oil. It flared bright orange.

Half-pint clung to Madame's skirt.

"A multitude of sins," said Churchy, slamming his Bible shut and then opening it again.

"If you don't want to watch, then go to your choir practice," said Madame. "General is leaving that chair tonight."

Churchy snapped his Bible shut and opened it again. He disappeared through the ceiling and strains of "When the Roll Is Called Up Yonder" wended their way.

"I smell smoke," said General.

"Maybe it's your guilty conscience for blowing cigar smoke in the baby's face," said Churchy, snapping his Bible shut and opening it again.

"How many times do I have to tell you to get lost?" asked General, looking up. "I think the smoke is coming from the hotel rooms. I'm going to blow some of it toward the telephone operator's booth so the telephone operator can sound the fire alarm."

"Just get up and go tell her," said Madame.

"Never," said General.

"Lazy," said Churchy. "You are my cross to bear."

"I'm no trouble to anyone *if* they leave me alone," said General, sending the smoke the operator's way.

"Fire, fire!" someone yelled from the hotel hall.

Half-pint blew in. "Let's get out of here."

Orange flames swept down the south wing hall. A vapor of smoke hung over the lobby. Passengers coughed and choked, retreating outside the station doors and down the stairs into the underground walkway toward the train tracks.

The telephone operator hit the alarm and called the fire station. Officials stumbled out of their upstairs offices into the lobby.

"Alert the mail room," the operator said to one official. "Run to the baggage wing and get everything outside," she told another.

Madame sat back and smiled. "Now this is the kind of trouble I'm talkin' about."

The waiter walked around the corner from the dining room. "What's going on?"

"Clear the eating area and kitchen," said the operator. "The Station's on fire."

The waiter turned. "Come on, we have to get the people to safety, and then save the equipment. I want all of it outside."

The sound of the fire trucks clanged down the street.

"Run!" yelled Half-pint. "We'll be burned up."

"You're shaking like a leaf," said General. "The fire won't reach this far. The trucks are pulling up right now. They'll have this out in a few minutes."

He settled further into his velvet chair. "This is better than a movie. Retirement—it's the life."

"Get out!" screamed Half-pint. "Now!"

Churchy took Half-pint by the arm and pulled him up through the roof. The flames leaped skyward. Ceiling timbers fell in on themselves.

Madame hovered just above the flames.

"The whole building's going down," cried Half-pint.

"We'll be safe," said Churchy. "After all, we're already dead."

"This is what happened to my brother and sister—my parents. We all died in our house fire."

"Let's head toward the south wing. It's still intact." Churchy snapped his Bible shut and opened it again. "This is a real baptism by fire."

Flames engorged the entire south wing and chomped into the center of the building like a giant insatiable monster.

"This will rout the General out," said Madame.

"We'll have to go get him," said Churchy. "He won't come on his own."

"Churchy and I will help you." Half-pint still shook.

"I can't ask you to go with me," said Madame.

"I'll go, even though I'm scared," said Half-pint. "Like you say, I'm already dead—can't get worse than that."

The three ghosts swam through the smoke to the lobby. Churchy got hold of General's right arm.

Madame got hold of the other. "We've come to get you out."

"Leave me," said the General. "This is my second death. Maybe I'll have nine lives like a cat."

Half-pint grabbed the General's left leg.

Flames skittered along the floor and underneath General's chair.

Churchy tugged. "Pull, Half-pint."

Madame yanked up. "You're comin' with us."

Half-pint pulled.

Slowly, General rose from his chair.

"I haven't been out of this seat for forty years," said General.

"It's about time," said Madame.

"There's a house of worship just a couple of blocks away." Churchy pointed. "A rock one on the corner. We'll go there."

"Not on your life," said General. "I'll go with Madame."

"Well, I'm not taking you to Madame's," said Churchy. "That's immoral."

"Why?" asked Madame.

"Just set me back down and let me burn then," said General.

"Quit arguing," said Half-pint. "Let's get out."

They rose above the burning room toward the clock tower as a large crack sounded. The great time piece broke and crashed to the floor.

"We just missed that," said Half-pint.

All four glanced at the flames. The puny stream of water from the fire hose didn't begin to quench the giant hungry monster that advanced, burning ember by burning ember.

They could see the telephone operator standing outside by the fire truck, drenched and shivering.

"Now this is what I call fun," said Madame. "I have you out of that chair so you can ghost up Two-Bit Street with me."

"Madame," said General, "I see that you have bested me in this card game. I'm yours."

Madame smiled. "All mine? That's delicious."

"My place of business got too hot to handle." General sidled up to Madame and put his arm around her. "But I do like some heat."

"About time," said Madame. "You should've come sooner."

"You're right," said General. "What was I thinking?"

"Get thee behind me, Satan," said Churchy.

"Goodness," said Madame, looking at Churchy. "A house divided against itself cannot stand."

Churchy stiffened.

The ghostly group settled down through the roof and second floor into Madame's abode.

"Is there somewhere for me to sit?" asked General.

"Bring him in here," said Madame. "I have just place in my parlor—a red velvet chair."

Churchy and Half-pint lowered General into the scarlet seat.

"Now gentlemen, I welcome you to my home."

"Say on, dear Madame," said General.

"Our calling in death is to scare the life out of our Two-Bit Street patrons," said Madame. "They expect it of us. Will we disappoint them?"

"Wolves in sheep's clothing," said Churchy.

"If we play our cards right and work together," said Madame, winking at General, "we can ghost up the entire street. Spooky is not made of small stuff like knocking out light bulbs and lifting skirts. We must bring terror to the hearts of the living— become legends."

"Legends?" General asked.

Madame turned to Churchy, her arm circling his waist and pulling him close. "You have the talent to convert souls to sing with the angels or help us ghost up this street." She kissed him on the lips. "You decide. Are you with us or not?"

Churchy stepped back. "I–I'll stay with you."

"Great." Madame whirled from Churchy to the General's lap, running her fingers through his hair.

She turned to Half-pint. "You're a brave boy."

Half-pint smiled.

"I've watched you and your mischief," said Madame. "You'll make a great part of this legend-making team."

"Wow!" said Half-pint. "A team. Like baseball."

Madame turned to all three of them. "Now, let's go get 'em boys."

"Legends in our own time," said General, leaping from his chair and twirling Madame around the room.

"Cast my bread upon the waters," said Churchy.

"Let's play ball!" said Half-pint.

10. The Dare

Vicki Droogsma

Sometimes vacated old buildings take on a different persona during the witching hour on Historic 25th Street...

It started with a dare. All the stories prompted it. 25th Street was riddled with them—tales of ghosts, prostitutes, smugglers, dealers, and criminals who used to inhabit the infamous street, and haunted the old buildings.

"You can hear them, you know," Rob said as he lounged on the sofa in his apartment.

"Hear what?" Tom asked from the easy chair. They'd been watching Ghost Hunters when Rob brought up the subject of 25th Street.

"The ghosts. They say if you walk down the street late at night, you can hear a popping sound on the sidewalk."

"What's it supposed to be?" Tom said, not really wanting to know.

"Beans."

"Beans? Really?"

"Really. I've been told hookers tossed beans out the windows to get the men's attention."

"Right, you don't really believe in ghosts." Tom stood up and went to the kitchen for a soda.

"I dare you to go see for yourself," Rob piped up from the sofa.

Tom stepped out of the car into the dark night. Snow crunched under foot as he walked along the sidewalk.

He refused to look over his shoulder, knowing he would see Rob looking smug and warm in the car. Snow fell on his nose and he wiped it off. *Some dare. Walk the length of 25th Street and back at midnight. Such a simple thing.*

At Union Station, passing the dead fountain, turned off for the winter, he looked up the street as he waited for the light to change.

He crossed and stopped in front of a building and read a sign relating to its historical significance. He peered into the window. A pile of boards, paint cans, and other construction odds and ends littered the floor. Beyond that, the room faded into darkness.

Something harder than snow fell on his head. He looked up thinking it was a drop of water from the roof. He felt another.

"Hey!" he called, but received no answer.

Again, he felt something fall on his head and heard soft laughter filter down from above.

He stepped back and looked up. The façade of the building loomed over him silently. The moon shone on the glass, but only darkness reflected back.

"Looking for someone, darlin'?"

Tom whirled around and nearly fell into the street. There, standing so close he could feel her icy breath on his face, was a beautiful woman.

She laughed as he tried to regain his composure and his footing. "My apologies," she said. "Come, it's cold out; let me make it up to you."

Although shaken at her sudden appearance, Tom eyed her retro dress hugging the curves of her gorgeous figure. He stared at her with his mouth gaping open as he felt himself drowning in the depths of her dark eyes. He struggled to break free from her gaze, but it was no use.

She beckoned him to follow her as she turned to a glass door. After entering, she stopped on the stairs and paused expectantly.

He paused only for a minute thinking of Rob sitting in the car, and how jealous he'd be to know Tom had been invited into this dazzling woman's apartment. He smiled and reached into his pocket to turn off his phone.

He followed her up the stairs to a sparsely-furnished room containing a fancy sofa, a pair of matching chairs, and a low coffee table with a tea set. The warm glow of several oil lamps and a few candles lit the room. *Very cozy.* He presumed the door in the far wall led to a bedroom. Lace curtains fluttered in the breeze from an open window.

"Would you like something to drink? I have tea, or would you prefer something stronger?"

"Um, not tea," he replied.

Retrieving a bottle and two glasses from a cupboard, she filled them with an amber liquid.

"Here we are." She handed him a glass.

He took a sip and nearly gagged on the strange taste. It reminded him of the moonshine his Uncle used to brew.

"Wow, that's strong." He choked.

She sipped hers, very politely, and gazed at him over the rim.

"Nice apartment you have here," he spoke into the silence. "Very vintage... "

"It's home," she replied. She walked to the window, setting her glass on the sill.

He set his glass on the table. The shadow of her glass on the sill was captured in the rectangle of moonlight on the floor. He looked up. She still stood at the window. He glanced at the floor again and saw the patch of moonlight, the shadow of the glass, but nothing more. He stared at the woman at the window. The curtains waved gently, but the few loose strands of her hair didn't move.

She turned to him, gliding closer.

He stood up and backed away. "I should go." He went to leave, but the door had become a mirror. He felt her icy breath on his neck, yet only his own reflection showed in the mirror. He whipped around and headed for the other door in the room.

"I don't want you to leave." She placed a cold hand on his arm.

He shivered at the touch and tried to pass her. He turned to the door, but she blocked him again.

"Excuse me."

"Stay!" she commanded.

He struggled to avoid her eyes, but she was too close. He stared into their depths, feeling himself drifting as if he floated in a dark sea. He ripped his eyes from hers.

She shrieked, as if furious to be disobeyed. He felt coldness wafting from her in waves now. He struggled to get to the door.

"I—I want to get out of here," he stammered.

Her laughter echoed around The sound was no longer warm; the room no longer cozy.

He ran to the door and threw it open. Her callous laughter followed him as he fell into an empty void.

"Tom! Tom! Wake up! Dude, are you okay?

"Huh... I... where'd she go?"

"Who?" Rob asked as he looked down at his friend with a worried look on his face.

"The woman... " Tom whispered. He lifted his head where he lay on the sidewalk, in the snow. He looked around frantically, blinking against the heavy snow flakes settling on his eyelashes. But all he could see through the falling snow was a deserted parking lot.

"Holy shit!" Rob said. "I called you several times on your cell phone, and I went up and down 25th Street looking for you. Then I find you behind this building, flat on your back."

Tom sat up straight. He rubbed the back of his head where he could feel a huge lump forming. His shoulder ached.

Rob helped him up. "What the hell happened?"

"You're not gonna believe me when I tell you."

II. A Recipe for Reclamation

Dimitria Van Leeuwen

What hides behind the windows of those closed-up old Victorian Mansions? And if walls could talk, what would they tell us? Often times someone buys one of these houses... a dream come true... or is it?

I fell in love with the house the moment it came into view.

"This one is at the high end of your price range, but it's a magnificent home." The realtor pulled his car up at the curb next to the white, decorative wrought-iron fence that defined the corner lot on 25th street.

I looked up at the two-story, Victorian-style house, which was painted a pale gray with white trim.

It must have been built early in the last century, but seemed well taken care of. The lawn was neatly cropped and laced with pretty autumn leaves that had fallen overnight. The trees around the house and down the street glowed bright orange, red, and yellow against the flawless blue sky.

"Why would someone sell this place?" I asked.

"The woman who owns this house is in her nineties, and has recently moved into a retirement home, just up the street in fact. Her only son has lived in Connecticut since he was in college. He seems quite happy about the idea of selling it. I guess he hasn't been back to Ogden, even to visit, for more than forty years."

"Well, I haven't been back in a while either," I smiled up at the blue sky. "When I was in school, I used to live in a little apartment just a few blocks from here. I used to daydream about someday having a house like this."

I didn't add that my roommate back then had been my twin sister, Lainie, and that I had taken a job out of town a year after she was killed in a skiing accident.

I could afford a house now. I had written a series of cookbooks spiced up by stories and anecdotes, mostly humorous. They were all about the love and fun of bringing friends and family together for a good meal. Although Lainie wasn't around anymore physically, I always seemed to feel her there in my imagination—laughing with me at the silly things in life—and I wrote her into many of my stories.

My books had each become best sellers, and were even doing well internationally. When I felt it was time to settle down, I was pulled back to the city where I grew up. As I smiled up at the house, I sensed Lainie was there beside me, smiling too.

"Let's go take a look inside," the realtor suggested, but I didn't even have to see it—I already knew this would be my home.

It was several weeks before I could finally move in. I'd had the kitchen entirely remodeled, while I repainted several rooms myself. Often I would step back to admire my work, and in my mind, I'd feel my sister beaming with approval.

Some personal items and furniture remained from the last owner, and her son had apparently communicated that he didn't want anything. There was no room for the belongings where his mother lived now. I moved it all to a corner in the basement until I could talk to the former owner to see what she wanted done with it.

I decided to go see her personally.

Her name was Florence Madsen. The modest single-story retirement home, Golden Hours Retirement Center, where she now lived, was on 25th street, not far from the house.

When I knocked, she opened the door and invited me in. Nodding involuntarily, she had a continual little bounce in her head and hands. I sat on the floral couch and told her why I'd come.

"Oh, I don't really care what you do with it all," she muttered. "I've kept most of Robert's things, but now I don't have anywhere to put them." She seemed a little distressed.

"Robert? Your husband?"

"My son…"

"Well, I guess he doesn't want any of his stuff if he hasn't seen it for this long."

She snorted. "No use for it where he is now."

I felt like I was missing the punch line, but I'm not really one to pry so I let it go. I told her I'd store her things in the basement while she was deciding what to do with them. After a few pleasantries, I said goodbye and let myself out.

I spent a day window shopping on 25th Street, near the Union Station. While looking at a beautiful scarf in one of the boutiques, I glanced out through the window and saw Lila, my new neighbor. She was a beautiful woman in her late sixties, who I felt could become a good friend. She seemed very wise, calm, and pleasant, with a touch of something mystical about her, despite her outdoorsy clothing and chin-length tidy gray hair. She'd grown up across the street from my new house. As we chatted, I asked her if she had known the people who had lived there previously.

"Oh, yes, the Madsen family, I've known them since I was a child. It's nice to see someone new move into that house. You're doing some remodeling, I hear?"

I excitedly told her about my new kitchen, and realized only later that she had avoided talking about the Madsens.

I'd been keeping so busy that the day of the anniversary of Lainie's accident almost snuck up on me. It always surprised me that I still felt the echoes of despair from something that had happened so many years ago.

The day arrived, and I didn't get out of bed. I just wanted to sleep through it. Thoughts of missing her brought thoughts of being alone, which brought memories of missed opportunities and mistakes I'd made.

I had worked myself into a fine ball of misery by evening, but I was getting hungry. I put on some jeans and a baseball cap and ran down the street to Grounds for Coffee on 25th street and then to the grocery store. By the time I got home, it was dark and cold and the house seemed to loom rather than to welcome me.

I walked in the front door and hesitated. Tonight, my new home seemed unpleasant. It was almost as if there was a bad smell in the air; the corners seemed a little darker. The old wood floor creaked. I stood with the keys still in my hand, but I could find no obvious reason for my unease, so I resolutely set about my evening, deciding to start the laundry before I made my dinner.

The laundry room was in a corner of the basement. The walls showed the old stone foundation, the floor was cement, and a single bulb hung from the end of a cord in the middle of the ceiling. This room was on my list of remodels for the following spring, but for now it didn't need to look pretty to get the job done. I quickly sorted clothing, wanting to finish and get out of that stifling room. More than once I turned and looked over my shoulder, feeling as if I was being watched.

As I added the detergent and set the dial on the washer, I noticed that the harsh shadows cast by the uncovered light were swaying slightly, and I wasn't sure if I was imagining it, but it seemed that they had begun to swing farther and farther out. Startled, I stepped back and looked up at the light, which was moving as if a hand had pushed it, pitching back and forth now, almost to the ceiling. Was this an earthquake? I felt my heart beating hard as I backed out of the room and shamelessly ran up the stairs, glancing back over my shoulder.

In the kitchen, I stood looking at the basement door, not sure what was going on. I just told myself to ignore the whole thing. That night, it took a long time to fall asleep, but in the morning the sun shone brightly into my bedroom, lighting up the pale blue walls. My fears from the night before seemed silly. It seemed I felt Lainie smiling at me again and the world seemed right.

I made a pot of tea and decided to sit in the living room with my laptop and get some work done. I was gazing out the large front window at the birds in the front yard, when I saw Lila, out for her morning walk.

I jumped up and opened my front door, calling out to her. She stopped with a smile as I jogged out to the gate.

"I wanted to ask you something," I spoke loudly over the cold wind as it blew my hair around wildly. I hugged my arms to my sides for warmth. "Did you feel an earthquake last night? Around 8:00?"

"No, honey, nothing. Did something happen?" She darted a look behind me at the house.

"No... I guess not." I felt a little self-conscious, and I must have looked it, because Lila changed the subject. "So, will you be visiting family for the holidays this year?"

"I don't think so." I paused, and then I told her, "After my sister died, my parents divorced, and now Mom's in Hawaii making pottery, and Dad is living in Oregon with a young new wife. Kind of a cliché." I smiled. "Actually, the new wife is very nice and I quite like her, but my dad feels like a stranger to me. All we ever manage these days is a strained politeness. So... really, I think I'll just keep my lovely new home all to myself this year.

"You should stop by for tea sometime," I said.

Lila looked a little surprised at my change of subject and it made me laugh. "No?" I teased her. "Coffee? Watermelon Martini?"

She smiled again now. "You're going to be just fine," she said, reaching over the rail to give me a quick hug, and I felt almost like she was reassuring herself as well as me, "You just keep smiling. And I'll stop by for that martini," she laughed.

A couple of pleasant and productive weeks passed, and the snow started to come down. Then one day, I realized Christmas was around the corner and I again found myself becoming melancholy.

Over the next few days, I got into quite a funk. Despite lots of cards and calls from many friends, I felt lost at the idea of being so alone on Christmas. My usual sense of humor at little everyday things evaporated, and even Lainie's cheerful background presence was missing. I fell into a spiral of unhappy thoughts.

One night I fell asleep with my bedside light still on, the book I'd been reading on my chest. I woke with a start; sure that someone had been standing over my bed, watching me.

I thought I'd try to call Lila, for a little company, but her machine picked up. I hung up without leaving a message. I kicked off my shoes, since I had no friends and wasn't going anywhere tonight, and decided to do housework.

I marched downstairs into the basement, feeling angry about my life. I glared at the pile of junk the Madsens had left. "I should just sell this crap, or throw it in the dumpster."

The dryer buzzer sounded loudly, startling me. My heart was still thumping as I pulled the hot clothes out into a basket.

"*No one loves you.*"

I straightened up and froze, listening. A harsh voice had just come loudly into my head—an intrusion. I strained to know if the sound had been physical. The echo of a man's cruel whisper rang in my head. I was stunned and terrified.

"*You're alone...*" The voice came again, in a tone that was mean and mocking.

I'm losing my mind, I thought. I yelled at the empty room, "Shut up!" I felt a sting on my cheek, and I reached up to find a thin line of blood had been scratched under my eye. I turned to the doorway and there was a dark shadow of a man, angry, hateful, and glaring at me with fury. I screamed, and for a moment, closed my eyes.

There was only an empty doorway when I looked again, and frantically I ran up the stairs and out my front door into the wet snow, and I didn't stop until I was on Lila's porch.

She opened the door and saw me in my stocking feet with blood on my face. She quickly pulled me inside. She sat me in her chair by the fire, tucked a soft throw around my shoulders, and had me pull off my wet socks while she went to get me some warm slippers and a cup of hot tea.

She sat beside me and said calmly, "Tell me."

She listened to my story, nodding, not seeming surprised. "I know there are some dark memories there," she told me. "Old houses have history and some of it not so good."

"Maybe it's their things that are still in house—pictures, clothes... " I gestured helplessly, "Florence said she'd kept all of Robert's things. I'm going to call him and make him take it all away."

Lila put her hand on mine and looked at me sympathetically. "Honey, Robert isn't the son that lives in Connecticut. Robert is her other son, the one that hung himself in the basement, forty years ago."

Lila gave me her take on things. "I knew Robert. He was an angry and unhappy person. He was mean to everyone around him, but most of his hatred was directed at himself. There are streams of thought, of emotion, of experience that still exist even after a person dies. They are all around us, both good and bad. Sometimes these streams are very intense, and can coalesce into something we can see or feel. But," Lila looked me in the eye. "We only experience that which we are in harmony with.

"It is *real*, if you define real as being something you can experience through your physical and emotional senses. But what I want you to remember, honey, is that your anger and fear is all that brought it to you, and all that keeps it with you. A smile and a thought of love instantly bring in light that pushes the edges of the dark away. The power is all yours."

That was a lot to take in, and I wasn't sure how I felt about her words, but I thanked her and accepted the offer to spend the night on her couch.

The next day, I was still afraid, but I had a plan. I couldn't stay on Lila's couch for the rest of my life.

And I wanted that house—my house.

It was quiet and sunny when I walked in. But things still didn't feel right. Still, I was okay until the sun went down, and then I began to jump at little noises and see a dark shadow just out of the corner of my eye. My fears had all surfaced again.

I decided to bake. I had a recipe for cinnamon apple dumplings that was divine, and I would bring some to Lila when I finished. I assembled the ingredients on my kitchen island and had measured the flour into a large mixing bowl. In another bowl, I broke several eggs, and was wiping my hands on my apron, when the door to the basement slammed shut right in front of my eyes.

Damn it. I had dreamed of having my own place like this for half my life. I was ready to battle for it if I had to. "I'm not giving it up!" I called into the echoing silence, and felt a responding anger in the air. The hair on my arms began to rise.

I continued with my baking. I found the hand-held eggbeater I'd had for years. Normally I found it pleasant to use all the old hand tools my mother had left me before she became a potter. I turned to the clock on the wall to check the time when I heard a terrible hissing sound. I whipped back around and as I watched, the bowl of flour began to shake slightly, then with a rush, slid off the counter, hit me, and crashed onto the floor. "*A smile and a*

164

thought of love…" I swear I heard Lainie repeat Lila's words, and I thought of those people who I loved so much, and who had always been with me.

I pushed the corners of my mouth into a fierce smile and whispered out loud, "I'm *not* alone and I'm sorry for you. I'm not afraid. I'm only sorry for you!" I spoke louder, "Lainie, I know you're here and I love you."

Tears of relief gathered in my eyes then spilled over. "And I know you are always there for me, when I let you be, and I know I am loved!"

Chills of affirmation ran through my body.

"I love Lila. She's a wonderful person, and a friend, and she loves me." With each word, energy ran through me, chasing the fear out of my veins. I took a deep breath, "And *I* love me. I am amazing, damn it!"

At this declaration, I turned and saw my reflection in the kitchen window—flour on half my face and in my hair, the egg beater raised defiantly in my hand. Was I going to chase down a ghost and get him with this thing? I giggled, picturing me turning the metal handle in quick threatening circles.

I laughed and cried with relief; my fear gone. I felt Lainie there again with me, I felt my power, and I smiled triumphantly with a sure knowledge that I had won my home.

Years later, the week before Christmas, I think back on my first year in this house—my house—and I realize how right Lila was. The power was always mine. And I stand in the glow of the Christmas lights, feeling the warmth of the fire, looking out through picture window at the reflected sparkle on the snow outside… and I smile.

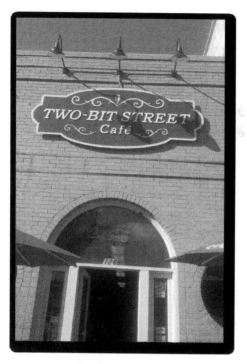

12. The Man in the Bowler Hat

Drienie Hattingh

The party was in full swing at Two-Bit Street Café. The owners, Penny and James, hosted the Italian night every year. Everyone dressed up Italian-style. Lots of men wore suits and hats that made them look like mafia bosses. Penny's excellent Italian fare, in platters, each more appetizing than the last, had been set throughout the restaurant to tempt the guests.

The restaurant was divided in two. The main entrance consisted of the long antique bar counter, some tables in the front and a couple of booths in the back. The other section, a deli with more booths, was located through an arch in the wall. The building dated back to the early 1900s, when Ogden was a so-called red light district.

I love these nights. This is how people should dress all the time—properly. Not like they dress the rest of the year. Damnation! The women who come in here to dine usually looks as though they are wearing sleepwear—those flimsy dresses. They look worse than the women who used to sell themselves on the street. And the men—a disgrace for the rest of mankind— dressed in those short pants and no socks or boots. Scandalous!

Earlier, as Penny prepared for the night and made all the traditional Italian dishes, she also made sure that the special bowl, in which she made the tiramisu every year, was sparkling clean. She loved this pretty glass bowl that she received as a gift from a dear friend when she and James opened the restaurant some years before. Somehow, the bowl became the one she used *only* for the Italian night.

Penny is different. She always dresses respectfully and lovely, in flowing attire, complementing her persona gracefully. She is like women should be, not exposing herself like those other women. And I do love her long auburn hair. Sometimes she wears it loose and it cascades right down to her back. Boy, if I was younger...

Penny reminds me of Momma, always in her place and working hard—like a good woman should—not like those young women on the street, smoking and wearing cut-up pants and coloring their hair and sometimes, it doesn't even look as though they brushed it before they left home. And I do not understand why they have the likeness of snakes and other abominations painted on their arms and legs.

Penny smiled as she moved through the happy guests. Dean Martin's voice filled the restaurant. As she topped up the punch bowl, she sang softly along, "When the world seems to shine like you've had too much wine, that's amore..."

When you walk down in a dream but you know you're not dreaming signore...
You're in love...That's amore!

Oh, Penny! We have so much in common, even the same taste in music. Dino! Just like ol' blue eyes and the rest of the gang. This, my dear Penny, is how every day should be. Good food, nicely dressed clients, and good music. Not the stuff that blares over the speakers on the street... well, sometimes the music on the street isn't that bad, I have to admit. I love the music over Christmas time.

"Penny! Hi!" a young woman from across the room called out. "The food is delicious."

Penny smiled and waved back. It was Sadie, the owner of Grounds for Coffee, located across the street. Just as with other events she catered, Penny wished she could stop and visit with locals and guests but as usual, even though she tried to prepare most of the food ahead of time, she spent the better part of the night in the kitchen. She could hardly believe it when she looked at the clock above the arch and saw that it was 10 o'clock. She heard James saying goodnight to the last diners as she carefully rinsed the tiramisu bowl and wiped it with a dry cloth till it shined. She twisted it to one side and then the other to watch it sparkle in the light from the bulb above her.

I love that bowl too, dearest Penny. Just look at it sparkle. It looks almost as lovely as

170

when the early morning sun strikes it just right, when it sparkles with all of the colors of the rainbow.

She helped the staff clean the restaurant. They swept the floors and put clean tablecloths on the tables for tomorrow's Sunday brunch. Penny carried the tiramisu bowl carefully to the deli section of the café and put it on the shelf, in its usual place. She stepped back and admired it. The intricate cut glass pattern shimmered. She walked to the arch, turned the lights off, leaving the area in darkness.

"Bye, Penny! See ya tomorrow," Diane, one of the waitresses, called from the front of the store.

Penny called back, "Bye!" and then heard the door click as Diane left. She picked up her purse, looked around the room one last time, and turned off the lights. She locked the door behind her and walked to the car where James waited.

Two weeks passed pleasantly enough, and one early Tuesday morning, Penny unlocked the front door of Two-Bit Street Café and walked in. She loved getting to the café early, before the others. The interior of the old restaurant seemed different, more soulful, to her this time of day. It was as though a gentle positive energy surrounded her which she felt sure was left there by those long-dead people who occupied this space before her.

I love it when Penny and I are the only people in the restaurant. I know she knows I am here. I can see it in the way she smiles. This is our time.

Penny hung up her coat and put her purse under the counter, as she did every morning. She walked through the arch leading to the deli with a smile on her face. She loved this place. It had been tough to keep it going, competing with all the other restaurants on 25th Street, but this café was her second home. This was where she could live out her passion of making people happy with her creative meals. Then she stopped dead in her tracks.

Right there, in front of her, on the wooden floor, was the glass tiramisu bowl. It just sat there— it wasn't broken or marred in any way—sparkling brightly in the early morning sun coming through the windows. The sunrays seem to land exactly on the spot where the bowl was.

Oh no! I forgot to put the bowl back. How could I have forgotten? It's because she is earlier today. . . Those early morning sunrays catch the bowl in just the right way making it sparkle. I'm glad she can see it at last. Perhaps she will know I put it there. She knows I'm here…. I know she knows. Look at her; she is looking at it like I do every morning. She can see how it sparkles in the sunlight. Perhaps she will come early every morning to enjoy the sparkling bowl with me.

Penny slowly walked over to the bowl, eyeing it from all angles. *I was the last one here last night and I'm the first one in the store today. How can this be? And even if someone did get in here, why in heaven's name would they put the bowl in the middle of the floor?*

Eventually, she bent down and picked up the bowl. She slowly walked over to the shelf and carefully put it back where it belonged. She moved it around a bit, trying to see if it was possible that it could have slid off the shelf, but it wasn't. The shelf was level and even a bit coarse. She turned around and walked back through the arch to the kitchen in the next room, shaking her head.

Penny mentioned the incident to James and Diane. They both shook their heads, saying, "There has to be a logical explanation." But they too could not figure out what it could be.

The next day Penny visited with a friend, during a quiet time in the café. While sitting at the bar, she told him what had happened.

He listened with interest and then said, with a smile, "Penny, you know how this street is just steeped in history and legends and ghosts. I think you have your very own ghost here!"

Penny laughed, "Don't be silly! I don't believe in ghosts. There has to be a logical expla—"

A huge crashing sound interrupted Penny, and she jumped up and looked toward the steel shelves in the corner, next to the bar. Her eyes widened in amazement and horror when she saw everything on the shelves—the salt and pepper shakers, the plates, the cups and saucers and silverware—come crashing down to the floor, as if someone swept them right off the shelves with an invisible arm.

While Penny looked at the shattered pieces on the ground, she said, with a strangled laugh, "Okay! I'm sorry. I believe in ghosts!"

That really hurt, Penny. I thought you knew about me and cared for me. And I'm not a common ghost. I'm a gentle, kind spirit. I cannot believe, after all these years... when I thought you and I... Well, never mind. I will have to make some decisions today.

I guess it's time for me to move on.

Penny's friend helped her clean up the mess.

Later that day, a snow storm moved in. Penny carried a carrot cake she had just finished icing into the deli and put it into the fridge. Everyone else had already left.

Penny put on her coat, twirled a scarf around her neck, and picked up her purse. She was about to turn the lights off when she saw a movement outside. It was one of those curiously bright snowy nights. Even though it was snowing and clouded over, the world outside seemed as bright as day.

Penny saw a man dressed in a bowler hat walking past the restaurant's window. He wore a tweed jacket and an umbrella was hooked over his arm. Absentmindedly, she wondered if there was something '20s going on at the station.

As she watched, the man lifted his hat to her and nodded. He did not smile and actually looked sad.

Goodbye, my dear. It's been a pleasure.

She nodded and smiled at him, but suddenly she felt a pang of recognition. *I know him...*

She rushed to the door and into the snowy night.

Penny looked up the street, toward the Union Station. The station and surrounding area was deserted and very quiet. There wasn't anyone on the bright, snow-filled sidewalk.

But the thing that made the hair stand up on Penny's neck was the fact that there weren't any footprints in the snow.

13. Yehudi

Doug Gibson

I t was only in her dreams that Patricia recalled the terrifying events of that hot, sweat-sticky July night at Union Station on 25th Street.

She'd wake up screaming, thinking, "Melting flesh... red eyes... *Yehudi*."

The memories would quickly evaporate, consigned to what she could recall when awake—a boring date at the Grand Lobby, and a boyfriend she desperately wanted to chuck, and eventually, upchucked on.

His name was Stephen—good looking, blonde hair, nice hazel eyes, and skin that hadn't turned earth-weathered red yet. He was a gym teacher at a high school. Sitting at the table, in the Grand Lobby, she surveyed him with a bored air, a faux smile plastered on her attractive face.

Patricia, a red-haired career student working on a dissertation in psychology that still seemed far away, had frankly enjoyed the sex that accompanied their second date, and beyond. "The sex *is* great," she silently spoke to herself, but Stephen was dull. He was a man who thought mostly about Tom Brady and the fortunes of the New England Patriots, Boston Celtics, Boston Bruins, or whatever sport was in season for a Massachusetts team.

Stephen had gone to school there—Boston College. One didn't ask Stephen what he thought of the situation in the Middle East, or whether Congress or the administration was responsible for the inertia over the budget. He didn't care, and why should he? *Who needs that information to watch teenagers do jumping jacks or climb ropes?* Patricia thought maliciously.

She knew that Stephen suspected that she suspected he was an airhead. But he was infatuated with her. In their non-sexual encounters, his facial expressions betrayed that desperation. They alternated between delight on his countenance, knowing he was with someone he loved, and jackrabbit-eyed despair. He knew she was bored by him and that she betrayed that boredom by not changing her placid smile for minutes amid slight nods, smiles that dip below the eyes, and the requisite "uh-huh."

And Stephen had become so predictable, hard body and handsome face notwithstanding. Patricia was attracted to psychology because of how unpredictable humans could be even if her textbooks and psychologist's manual said otherwise. She loved the surprise of seeing someone do something out of the ordinary. The more mysterious or bizarre, the more intriguing the subject was to her.

And Stephen seemed to have so few emotions, mostly bland. And wow, it was hot and stuffy tonight at this fundraiser for the United Way. Stephen had secured the tickets for this. The food was the usual: chicken with lukewarm cream, cold vegetables, a hard roll with a pat of butter, Wal-Mart soda disguised in a classy glass, and a tasty flan for dessert. But it was oppressive, with 300 bodies in a lobby that once served as a train station. The high ceiling's potential for coolness was neutralized by the closed windows above. Sweat formed at various points of Patricia's body under her best dress. She noticed sweat sliding down the corner of Stephen's left eye.

"Let's dance," said Stephen. Dessert was over, and the band was playing. Several couples were moving slowly on a dance floor formed in the middle of the lobby, surrounded by tables.

Patricia upped her faux smile and shook her head. She grabbed a bottle of ice water and pressed it against her forehead. She leaned forward, and with the confidence of an intimate, pressed the glass against his left eye, wiping away the sweat stream.

Stephen blinked, ran his hand up through his sweaty hair. "I could use some more water," he said and took off.

Surveying the lobby scene, Patricia noted with interest a woman at the far left side of the lobby. She was dressed oddly, in a skirt that extended to her ankles and a high-button blouse. *How strange*, she thought. The woman appeared to take no interest in the desultory charity proceedings. Indeed, she was staring intently at a portion of the wall. A train whistle suddenly broke the low murmur of the lobby. Patricia jumped at the unexpected sound.

The woman turned and looked directly at Patricia, with a knowing glance. Patricia felt a not unwelcome chill.

What occurred next caused her to blink several times. A man with a cape seemed to appear from nowhere. He grabbed the woman and kissed her. Far from greeting him, the woman slapped the man, who backed away and disappeared. Patricia closed her eyes, shook her head, and opened her eyes. Both the woman and man were gone. The pleasant coolness she had felt was also gone.

I'm getting sick... hallucinating, thought Patricia, who started to feel nauseated. The short-lived cold spell had ceased and now her forehead again began to sweat. She was breathing heavily, the taste of bad chicken lodged just below her throat. She saw Stephen walking slowly, a glass of water in his hand, maneuvering between tables.

"Must get away to a bathroom," she thought. She waved palms up to Stephen in a no-need-to-follow-me gesture and pushed her chair out. She staggered into a table. Dripping with sweat, she waved off faces both irritated and concerned. Dizzy, she headed toward the dance floor, which had thinned to two pairs. She hoped she wouldn't vomit.

An unfamiliar hand grabbed her. It was almost icy cold, but refreshing. At that precise moment, Patricia's nausea and fever vanished. It was no longer sticky and hot. Everything was cold now—perhaps too cold—but it felt so good.

Patricia, following her rescuer's lead, her hand in his, collided with a heavyset woman and a little boy the fat woman was half-leading, half-dragging across the lobby floor. The United Way event had disappeared. The woman, in her thirties, was wearing a gingham dress to her ankles that looked the worse for wear. Her hair was faded brown with the beginnings of gray at the temples. She scowled at Patricia as she reached for her charge, a chunky towhead, perhaps thirty pounds and dressed in overalls. He was bawling.

"What's the matter with you? You almost scared Timmy to death." Her attention shifted to the boy. "Don't cry, Timmy. Daddy's arriving soon on the five o'clock," she cooed.

Patricia understood that the lobby had changed. She might have been more concerned if she wasn't feeling so much better. The sickness was gone. In the Grand Lobby, scores of people were seated, standing, or talking at various desks and tables. There were timetables on the wall. She glanced at the owner of the hand that was guiding her, pushing her through the room. She knew he was the man she had seen being rebuffed by the oddly-dressed woman just a few minutes ago. He was more than well-dressed, with a top hat and the wide cape. He wore an old-fashioned detachable collar. The brim of the hat covered his eyes. His black hair obscured his forehead. He had a wide wax-like mustache.

It dawned on her that she must have fainted. This is a hallucination.

For a brief second, Patricia thought she saw Stephen with a concerned look on his face. The nausea returned and then disappeared along with Stephen's face.

"Who are you?" she asked, turning to the man. They were yards from the exit of the lobby.

"Yehudi" was the answer she received.

Outside the lobby, snow was falling. The air was cool and the white snow provided a soft glitter more pleasing than the sun. Ogden's 25th Street didn't look like the Ogden she knew. The lights that separated Two-Bit Street from the train station were gone. Tracks ran through the middle of the street, making it seem thinner. She followed Yehudi down a street that boasted canopies as far as she could see. She passed a hotel, took a quick glance to her left, and saw only brown and black faces by the desk and in the lobby.

Patricia was an intelligent woman. She knew this wasn't real. Stephen's worrying face, as well as her nausea and sweating, would return soon enough. She settled back to enjoy this bizarre dream and the icy coolness. With her hand in Yehudi's, she drifted down the street, not even sure if her feet were touching the walkways. Her guide led her with a determined air, as if he had a specific destination.

On the wall of a passing restaurant was a sign advertising a prizefighting match at The Armory between Jack Dempsey, also known as Kid Blackie, and The Boston Bearcat. It was scheduled for

February 23. Patricia had only a vague idea who Jack Dempsey was, but she now knew why it was cold. It was February here. On the corner, a boy in an apron hawked newspapers.

She pulled at Yehudi. *I want to see what year it is*, she thought. He stopped with a grimace. In a single instant, he turned her body around and then closer to him. Patricia's hair was against his lips. He blew a gentle, icy breeze that passed into her right ear. His hands gently massaged her hips. Patricia ceased to care what date was on the newspaper. Yehudi took her hand and they continued on his path.

They passed where she heard Jack Dempsey and The Boston Bearcat speaking to the crowd about their future fight. How she knew it was them she couldn't have explained.

Something from the skies grazed her head. Still moving steadily, she looked up and saw a female face at a window. She sensed a leer from Yehudi directed at the woman. For the first time, Patricia felt a little uneasy.

Her eyes shifted to the right. A man stumbled across the street in her direction. His path led from another saloon. There are so many bars in Patricia's new 25th Street. The man staggered toward her on the sidewalk, clearly intoxicated.

"Hey, little lady," he slurred. "You 'bout the prettiest darling I've seen today. I sorry for my 'peerance." The drunk attempted to grab Patricia's free arm. She shrank away.

Yehudi, who took no notice of the drunk, kept her a step ahead of the bum, who was wearing a ragged coat, a stained white shirt with no collar, and crushed stove-top hat.

Patricia heard a bump, a curse, and a thud. The drunk had stumbled into a large cigar store Indian. He ceased to follow her.

Yehudi finally stopped in front of a corner building. Patricia noticed a sign that said, "Arcade." He pulled her inside. In the entrance, stood what would be a very old machine today. It was a crystal ball with a mechanical grandmother leaning over it. "Learn your fortune" read the inscription on the machine.

A penny was in Patricia's hand. Yehudi was behind her, gently massaging her neck. She inserted the penny, and a jingle was heard from the fortune machine. A slip of paper dropped into a tiny attached basket. Patricia grabbed it.

"Yehudi. Yehudi. Yehudi. Love Yehudi" was all the slip of paper said.

Patricia felt her body being turned toward her companion. She faced him with his chin lowered, his brow still obscuring most of his face. As he moved his lips toward her mouth, Patricia closed her eyes and anticipated the kiss. Fear tingled through her, but so did anticipation.

When their lips touched, she recoiled in horror. His kiss tasted like a charnel house. Gagging, she expelled a sickly, sour gas from her mouth. She pushed back, but his hands had tightened on her shoulders and his ghastly breath and taste entered her mouth again. Panicked, she bit at his lips. It opened its mouth wide, temporarily freeing her.

Patricia screamed at what she saw. Above the mustache, Yehudi's face was melting. The eyes joined the cheeks. The forehead was bubbly, a mountain of craters and pus-filled sacks. The top half of its nose appeared to be eaten. It smiled through clenched teeth that were black with decay. The lips were slit and blackened, crusted blood was stained with Patricia's lipstick.

"Yehudi fooled you!" it hissed and then giggled.

Patricia screamed again and staggered out of the arcade. For a brief second, she saw Stephen's face along with others. "Wake up," she begged.

"No, no, Yehudi says no. Take you upstairs." The thing ambled toward her.

Patricia turned to run, but dreamlike, she couldn't move fast enough. It clamped its hand onto her forearm.

"Lots more for us to see. Go upstairs, be my girl, go to fight, see Dempsey," it cackled.

Patricia had an overwhelming moment of despair.

"No, Yehudi, that's enough," said a voice.

Yehudi stopped.

Patricia stumbled into it and gagged on its moth-ridden, stained, age-stinking cape that had just a little while ago looked so new. The apparition took off, jerking down 25th Street. In what seemed like seconds, it was back at the train station.

Patricia shivered in fear as a new apparition approached. It was the woman she had seen in the Grand Lobby, the one who had once slapped Yehudi away. She was pretty, with a kind face that seemed a bit too motherly for a woman of her young age.

"He's harmless," she said. "A boozy flirt that can't maintain a conversation with a woman, so he turns into a monster you live ones see in the flickers you enjoy. Usually, he's only good for a parlor trick or two, but you appear to be more in tune with our generation," she continued, as she guided Patricia back down the street.

Things were changing. When she wasn't looking at the woman, it was 2013 again—hot and nighttime. Patricia's stomach lurched. But when she turned back to the woman, it was the old 25th Street. She caught a glimpse of the

Dempsey/Bearcat fight poster again.

"When Yehudi can find a human who can see us and is a bit gullible, he can become more than a nuisance. And let's face it, dearie, you were gullible. Must not have been too happy where you were tonight," she mused. "A word of advice: try to be happy around 'Two-Bit Street.'"

The woman took her hand and Patricia did what she thought was the most reasonable. She kept her eyes closed the rest of the journey back. Sometimes she felt her protector's hand. Sometimes she heard a voice or two.

Eventually, she opened her eyes. It was 2013, on a hot July night, in the Grand Lobby. She was huddled against the east wall, her head lolling on her shoulder. Stephen was in front of her, holding three paper napkins drenched in cold water to her forehead. A score of persons were behind him, looking on with excitable concern.

"Are you Okay, my love?" he asked.

Feeling hot and sick, she nevertheless nodded and mouthed, "Yes."

Suddenly, she felt cool again, and that chill moved through her body. She looked up.

Yehudi was at the top of the west side wall of the lobby. He had flung the window open. His chin was up. He was no longer melting, but his eyes were bright red. Patricia flung her own eyes down in horror. She was staring at the calves of a fat traveling salesman lugging his valise which she, for some reason, knew contained neckties that he peddled to storekeepers. He looked surprised to see Patricia appear at his ankles.

Patricia let out a piercing scream.

"Oh Yehudi! Cut the nonsense, or you'll be haunting the basement for the next ten years," yelled the woman, Patricia's protector.

As the man's trousers materialized into Stephen's worried face, an exhausted, terrified, very sick Patricia vomited all over her boyfriend's countenance.

Not long afterward, Stephen begged her to return to Grand Lobby for a school fund-raising function, and Patricia broke up with him.

Still, Patricia was often seen on 25th Street, and no doubt recognized by more than just the live ones of Two-Bit Street.

Truth be told, she occasionally saw an individual whose presence could change the weather for her. She stayed away from Union Station, though.

Once she stared at it from a safe distance and thought she saw an unfamiliar man, peering at her through a window. His eyes gleamed red. She clenched her eyes shut.

When she opened them, all was fine.

Acknowledgements

My sincere thanks go to the talented authors in this book. It would not have been possible if not for you—Christy, Dimitria, Doug, Fred, Lynda, Michele, Mike, Patricia and Vicki. Your creative writing and research shine through the retelling of these legends. You <u>are</u> storytellers!

Thanks to the business proprietors and '**the others**' on Historic 25th Street, who willingly shared their haunting tales with us, and in so doing, enabled us to write the stories in this spooky little book. After reading this second book in the series, residents of Ogden and beyond might look a bit differently at their surroundings—especially on dark and stormy nights.

Blessings to the Writing Divas—thank you my dear friends for your loving support, especially during the last months before this book was published. You are a blessing to me.

My everlasting love and gratitude goes to Johan who's always supportive in my endeavors even if they don't always make any sense *at all*.

Kudos to Janet Battisti, Carolyn Campbell, Heather B. Moore, and Barbara Passaris who took time from their extremely busy lives to review this book. You are amazing. Thank you!

My very best wishes go with Lynda West Scott, my partner in crime for the last two years, and who now lives in California. Why? Well, she had to choose between snow and the ocean. Thank you, Lynda, for going out on a limb and working with me on the first book in this series. I will always remember our times at Mad Moose Café spending whole days, morning till dusk, working on perfecting the stories. Keep on writing!

Love always to Wendy Toliver whose encouragement makes me believe I can write and that dreams do come true.

As so often, I must thank my daughter, Brenda, who stepped in at the last minute and edited one of the stories in this book! I love you and thanks for always being there for me.

My heartfelt gratitude goes to my long-time friend Dimitria Van Leeuwen, who read through the stories with me and brainstorming as we did. I will always remember that dark and stormy night (so fitting) reading, editing, until early morning hours.

Your keen sense for mystery and intrigue matches mine, and we could quite possibly commit the perfect crime—in a book—that is.

Many thanks to Amy and Les at DMT Publishers for your help and guidance in publishing 'the scary little books that could.'

Cheers to fellow South African, Stan Trollip for writing the introduction to this book (in the Swiss Alps, no less!) and for all your encouragement and support. Best of luck to you and Michael and I wish for the continued success for your Detective Kubu series! You are a wonderful example to all of us who are striving to become successful authors.

To our readers: *Thank you for buying this book. I hope you enjoyed the stories in this book, as much, if not more, than those in the previous book!*

Drienie Hattingh

About the Authors

Drienie Hattingh was born and raised in South Africa. She and her husband, Johan, and three children, Eugene, Brenda, and Yolandi immigrated to America in 1987. Drienie is a columnist and her articles and interviews (1,200) have been published in newspapers and magazines in America and South Africa. She is the author of an historical novel, *Forever Friends,* a novella, *A Glass Slipper for Christmas*, and her short stories are published in *Christmas Miracles, The Spirit of Christmas, Hallmark Gift Book: Christmas Miracles, Chicken Soup for the Soul: Be positive for Kids and the TALES series.* Drienie compiled and published the *TALES* series. When she's not writing, she loves to knit and travel with Johan and visit their children and grandsons, Simon and Tristan in Washington State and California. They also love to visit family and friends overseas. Drienie and Johan live in Ogden, Utah. Drienie is a member of the League of Utah Writers and The Writing Divas.

DrienieM@aol.com

Patricia Bossano author of award-winning Faery Sight and Cradle Gift (released soon) is of Ecuadorian descent. Having nurtured a love of languages, she taught Spanish and ESL and is also a translator and interpreter. She lives in Northern Utah with her two children. Her time is spent with family and indulging her passion in writing.

*Visit Patricia at: **http://www.patriciabossano.com***

Michael Bourn author of One Dead Ranger, released November 2012. He writes fiction and poetry, and spends a lot of time outdoors, biking and alpine and Nordic skiing. He's also an avid reader, a dabbler in watercolor, and a woodworker. Michael and his wife Pat live in Ogden, Utah at the mouth of beautiful Ogden Canyon. He is a member of The League of Utah Writers.

*You can contact Mike at **mrbourn@gmail.com***

Vicki Droogsma was born in England, and raised in California. She now lives in Ogden, Utah with her husband, two children, her cat and two guinea pigs. She loves writing.

You can contact Vicki at
Viledra@yahoo.com

Doug Gibson is the editorial page editor for the Standard-Examiner, a daily newspaper based in Ogden, Utah. Doug's been at the Standard Examiner since 1997. He's a native of Long Beach, CA, and a graduate of Brigham Young University. He has been a journalist for more than 20 years. He also taught journalism for two years as an adjunct at the University of Utah. He enjoys writing fiction, and has completed several short stories and one unpublished novel. He lives in Ogden with his wife, Kati, and three children. He loves ghost towns, Ogden history, ghost stories and tales that involve the dead coming back to life.

You can contact Doug at ***doug1963@gmail.com***

Michele   McKinnon graduated from Weber State University with a Master's degree in Accounting. She has been an avid reader all her life and lately turned her love of the written word into her own writing. Besides reading, writing and working, Michele loves gardening and playing with her grandkids. She lives in Bountiful, Utah near her children and grandchildren. She is a member of the League of Utah Writers and The Writing Divas.

You can contact Michele at
michele_mckinnon@yahoo.com

Christy Monson has worked as a Licensed Marriage and Family Therapist. She has written a children's book series, *Texting Through Time*, and has a self-help book, *Becoming Free, A Woman's Guide to Internal Strength*, to be released fall of 2013. Her articles have been published on the web in Familius, Gospel Ideals, LDS Witness, and Modern Molly Mormon.

Her blog address is:
http://christymonson.blogspot.com
Websites: **http://www.christymonson.com/index.html**
http://textingthroughtime.com
http://www.facebook.com/christymonsonauthor

Lynda West Scott worked as a private investigator for 25 years. Since then she has written magazine articles and worked as a copy editor. One of her essays appear in _Lessons From My Parents_ and two stories in _Tales from Huntsville, Eden, Liberty and Beyond..._ and two in _Tales from Two-Bit Street and Beyond... Part I._ She, along with Drienie Hattingh, edited, compiled and published the first two books in the TALES FROM H.E.L. series. Lynda and her husband, Mike, recently moved from Utah to California, to be closer to their grandchildren.

_Contact Lynda at **lynda_scott@msn.com**_

Fred Seppi, a lifelong resident of Ogden, Utah, received degrees in physics from Northwestern University and in metallurgical engineering from Illinois Institute of Technology. After retiring from Hill Air Force Base in 1986, where he'd worked as a physicist, he devoted himself to studying Italian and to creative writing. Several of his articles have appeared in the magazine _In Piazza_, published by the Italian Cultural Center of Utah, and he has recently completed a memoir, _The Boy under the Stairs._

Dimtiria Van Leeuwen has a varied background, including experience as a belly-dance teacher, musician, photographer, singing telegram messenger, and mixed-media artist. She is one of the lead singers in the band, SugarTown Alley. One of her stories, "Jelly," was published in *Tales from Huntsville, Eden, Liberty and Beyond...* Another one of her stories, "Kitten" was published in *Tales from Two-Bit Street and Beyond... Part I.*

You can contact Dimitria at **dimitria.vl@gmail.com**

In remembrance of Fred Seppi (1930-2015)

Fred was a kind and gentle soul who loved Historic 25th Street with a passion. He was a life-long resident of Ogden, Utah. Fred loved to tell people that he 'grew up' on 25th Street, during the so-called rough days. He did not remember the street as "rough." To him, it was populated by families who worked and lived on this street and earned their living the right way, by working hard. These families also, according to Fred, "looked out for each other."

Fred's father (known as Freddie) was the owner of *The National Tavern* on 25th Street (today known as Brewski's.) Fred was the janitor, who's job included polishing the bar counter to a shine. This janitor eventually received degrees in Physics from Northwestern University and Metallurgical engineering from Illinois Institute of Technology.

After retiring from Hill Air Force Base in 1986, where he worked as a physicist, he devoted himself to studying Italian and creative writing. Several of his articles have appeared in the magazine, Piazza, published by the Italian Cultural Center of Utah, and he recently completed a memoir, *The Boy Under the Porch.*

Fred's short story, *Goodbye Mary Belle,* was featured in *Tales from Two-Bit Street and Beyond, Part II,* published in June of 2013.

Photo Credits

The authors of Two-Bit Street and Beyond, Part II at the book launch at Two-Bit Street Café, on Historic 25th Street, Ogden.

Michele McKinnon, Doug Gibson, Vicki Droogsma, Drienie Hattingh, Lynda Scott, Dimitria VanLeeuwen, Patricia Bossano, Mike Bourn and Fred Seppi.

Absent from photo: Christy Monson.

Photo Credit: Mr. Droogsma

***I hope you enjoyed another spooky walk down
Two-Bit Street!***

To order more copies of *Tales from Two-Bit Street
and Beyond... Part I and Part II,* please email me
at: **DrienieM@aol.com.**

The authors in this book would love to hear your
thoughts on their stories. Please leave a review on
Amazon.

Thank you!

Tales from Beyond Series

Tales from Two-Bit Street and Beyond...Part I
Summer 2012

Tales from Two-Bit Street and Beyond...Part II
Summer 2013

Tales from the Wasatch and Beyond...
Summer 2014

Tales from Ogden Canyon and Beyond...
Fall 2016

Mineral Gray / Truck
Suv. Color

Wall Sconce / Eagles
Order to Ship by Wed, Jan 24TH
(11-30-17)

66464237R00118

Made in the USA
Charleston, SC
19 January 2017